THE BEST
HOUSE IN
STRATFORD

THE SILVER FALCON

Shakespeare & Son
Love's Labour's Won
The Best House in Stratford

EDWARD FISHER

The Best House In Stratford

ABELARD-SCHUMAN
London New York Toronto

London	*New York*	*Toronto*
Abelard-Schuman	Abelard-Schuman	Abelard-Schuman
Limited	Limited	Canada Limited
8 King St. WC2	6 West 57th St.	896 Queen St. W.

Printed in the United States of America

To the best and dearest of sisters
SISTER M. PHILIPPA

CONTENTS

Tell me, now,
If ever there was anything let loose
On earth by gods or devils heretofore
Like this mad, careful, proud, indifferent Shakespeare!
Where was it, if it ever was? By heaven,
'Twas never yet in Rhodes or Pergamon —
In Thebes or Nineveh, a thing like this!
No thing like this was ever out of England;
And that he knows. I wonder if he cares.
Perhaps he does. . . . O Lord, that House in Stratford!

— Edwin Arlington Robinson,
Ben Jonson Entertains a Man from Stratford

Book One

A LION

AMONG

LADIES

A lion among ladies is
a most dreadful thing;
for there is not a more
fearful wildfowl than
your lion living.

A Midsummer Night's Dream,
III, I.

chapter one

🎵🎵 SHOUTS and curses rose on the mildly blowing air. It was a morning in January, 1596, that notable mild month when roses bloomed in London.

A twittering of sparrows in the eaves of the Rose playhouse ceased, and all the birds flew away. The stage door thumped open. Out tumbled a bad actor, rolling and howling, his mad red hair like a fire needing to be quenched in a ditch.

"And stay out, bricklayer!"

Slam went the door. A party of watermen passed down Maiden Lane without giving him a curse. Here in Southwark, on the Bankside, one brawl more or one actor less hardly mattered. Still cursing, the rejected actor coughed out his last epithets.

A master of vituperation!

The bad actor displayed his splendid education by not repeating himself once.

Big-headed, lean-cheeked, hollow-eyed, with pockmarks all over his face, he sounded as though he might play an excellent murderer or a devil.

As he crawled out of the ditch and shook himself like a dog, he was still· eloquently cursing old Money-hugger Henslowe

15

and his glavering, goggle-eyed players who should be flayed of the foul and infected skin that held their squalid spirits in those abominable prison-houses of loathsome flesh. Hang and burn them all, and their cobbling play-makers with 'em.

"I'll leave these foul and infected precincts forever. What have I to do with these sneaking poets who barter their scurvy spirits for tainted shillings from a pawnbroker?"

A mangy dog, scavenging in a midden heap, began barking at him.

"What have I, Ben Jonson, descendant of Scottish lords and gentry, to do with such parcel-poets as these, who all write for sinners in the suburbs?"

"Bow wow wow!" said the dog.

Ben Jonson heaved a clod at him.

Then he carefully inspected his peculiar garment, a long cloak such as coachmen wore to protect them from rain and snow. Three or four shades of dirt, over a ground of gooseturd green, this extraordinary cloak covered him from head to heels. And it had large pockets sewn into the lining, very good and useful to a thief or a starving scholar, who could carry his few remaining books about with him from ditch to ditch, or perhaps his bad verses and rejected plays.

Young Jonson took a crust of bread and a piece of mouldy cheese from one pocket, and *The Odes of Horace* from another.

Feeding his stomach upon the bread and cheese and his brain upon his favourite poet, he began to feel quite cheerful.

"I'll be revenged on all my enemies before this year is out, I swear by Apollo."

He breathed in the free air and laughed to be still alive. Warm breezes, laden with the good smell of tar and brine, blew sweetly on him from the silver Thames. Fair shining sails rode past him on the tide, there was music on the water, and this world still had a few promises to offer a young man full of juice, talent, and a permanent hunger for glory.

"They cannot keep me down much longer," he muttered.

What if a searching rain fell on him from this sky again? It was the rain of England, mother of poets and heroes, and he was one of each.

"I've killed my man before two armies drawn up to see me do it in Flanders, and I'll be champion here too among the Bishop of Winchester's bawdy houses, ay, and in the Court at Westminster. And the same language will be suitable in both places."

What shall be my motto?

He pondered, scratching his starved cheeks, as full of eye-let-holes as a warming pan, which would not sprout a beard although he spent hours anointing them, and composing long classical incantations. A feeble sun-ray peeped through the mist and lighted up his wild tangled locks, making them even more frightful.

I have heard that this Shakespeare of theirs has tried to buy himself a coat of arms at the Heralds' College for thirty pounds.

Hang him for his little wit and his small learning! He steals all his plots from scurvy sixpenny pamphlets and Italian bawdy tales.

Ah, that a man like me, a classical scholar, a genius in his own right, should be kept down in this scurvy world of fawning parcel-poets, when all the treasure of Greece and Rome lies ready-minted in my brain!

Oh, what a world, that has no justice in it!

Poverty, poverty, poverty are the three words of my motto. And for my arms, my own sword and dagger.

As soon as I have ransomed them from old Pawnbroker Henslowe.

What if I try the Chamberlain's Men at their Curtain play-house in Shoreditch?

I could patch up their old plays as well or better than Shakespeare.

Hang him for his bad verses! They are as full of errors as a beggar's cloak is of fleas.

What's more, until Mr. Langley finishes his new Swan, I hear the Chamberlain's Men will be rehearsing at the Curtain.

As for Shakespeare, I can overlook their Shakespeare. I need not deign to stoop to their Shakespeare. I scorn their Shakespeare.

If I do not prove I am a better poet than their precious Shakespeare, yea, and ere the year's out, may I be hanged.

His long, thin, twisted nose, like the beak of some bird, sniffed the fragrant breeze blowing over the Thames. Flutes and fiddles played, and there was the far-off thrilling cry of silver trumpets, unmistakable to anyone who had ever heard them before.

Her Majesty is in her barge again, setting out to be entertained and banqueted in some precious noble's house. Thus will she even a little the balance owing to her from these sprouts of fortune she has suffered by her good pleasure to grow.

Ah God, what if she's to see another play by this unescapable Shakespeare?

He began to sweat with indignation at such injustice.

I would be at home here, I would be a happy man, if my enemies had only accorded me what is my due. And now, what do I hear?

His hot eyes, set crookedly under craggy brows, glared at the innocent white faces of the Bishop of Winchester's bawdy houses, from the Boar's Head to the Bell, the Crane to the Crosskeys, the Cardinal's Hat to the Gun.

Ah, you pretty fools, how I will miss you!

But there was clearly no justice extant. That upstart, lame-brained, small-witted son of a Stratford peasant would soon usurp this arena too.

Plainly to Ben Jonson's ears came the sound of hammers. They were working on it now, the scene of the unlettered countryman's future triumphs. Already its high tiled roof, with the flagstaff already mounted on the roof of the playing penthouse, rose nakedly over the chimney pots of watermen's houses, stews, taverns, alehouses, and the four gaols of

Southwark. In the best location too, just south of Paris Garden Stairs. And over the great entrance door, whose maw loomed open, they had set up a symbol for their new master — a swan.

Such insolence, to come crowding in here with his vulgar plays, when he had all the boobies of London and Shoreditch, the Smithfield whores, the carters and butchers and fishmongers and their apprentices from every shop in the city, as well as the feather-headed gentlemen from the Inns of Court, not to speak of the light ladies of the town! Two playhouses in Shoreditch, and another one leased in Blackfriars!

Such greed deserves retaliation and revenge by every educated playwright in Southwark. We should band together to say to this Shakespeare —

He forgot what the educated playwrights of Southwark should say to that Shakespeare. He brushed his awful cloak again, nodded his big head, which seemed to have been jammed on sideways in a hurry and pushed out of shape in the process.

"I'll go ask, anyhow," he muttered, his lower lip trembling.

And he went limping down Maid Lane until he came to the great yawning entrance door of the new Swan playhouse, the greatest, richest theatre yet to be built anywhere in England.

And damn all rich, including Mr. Francis Langley the trafficker in gold, who must have spent enough money on this new whale to keep me and my poor shrew in food, drink and lodgings for the rest of our lives. With a manor and land thrown into the scale, and horses too, and rich clothing, and a banqueting hall where the Queen might come to visit us.

Like some strange wild bird investigating a new horrible work of man in that innocent woodland which was his home, the lonely and hungry poet darted into the dark interior, shaded by the great galleries which ran all round the inner shell of the house, leaving a pool of gray daylight in the centre.

Planks and scantlings lay everywhere. Chunks of lime and plaster were sprinkled upon them. Workmen perched upon crosspieces and joined timbers in swimming air.

Trembling and on tiptoe, he cautiously picked his way

among the beams until he reached the stage. Ah, a quadrangular stage, this one. High as my heart. Paled in with good oak. Oh excellent fragrance of new wood! He bent to sniff at it. Heavy pillars to sustain the heavens, or the penthouse roof with all its gear above. No rails surrounding this stage. Forty paces by thirty.

He was trembling harder now, feeling the well-turned posts that supported the fronts of the galleries. He squinted up at the fit and decent boxes where the gentlemen would sit. They were ceiled already with lath and plaster, all good honest work of which a man could be proud. Good, good, delicious, that smell of fresh lime and new plaster-work.

Grunting with satisfaction, breathing it in, he wandered about in this lovely place, nodding his big ugly head.

And here, right here on this noble stage, it would be time for the play to begin.

Who is this first speaker, the Prologue?

Nobly handsome, manly, pleasing to women and winning the respect of gentlemen, he came forward proudly and began.

> "Nobles and gentles, you shall see today
> No monstrous follies, as you used to do,
> But deeds, and language such as men do use
> Writ by a man to show an image of our times
> And sport with human follies, not with crimes — "

Something cold, thick and wet hit him right in the mouth. Laughter rang in his ears. He staggered, choking, and fell over a pile of bricks in the playhouse yard.

"Away, you mouldy rogue!" yelled a voice from on high.

Ben Jonson got to his hands and knees, spitting out the mouthful of wet plaster. He reached for a brick and got it in both hands. He felt for a sharp stone, and tapped the brick against it. Now he had half a brick in each hand.

Up there, swinging like an ape from a rope ladder, a grinning plasterer scooped up another trowelful of wet plaster and flicked it down into his face, just as Ben looked up.

A chorus of laughter from all the workmen above.

The ragged poet stood up and began walking unsteadily toward the great entrance door.

Yells of triumph from above him all the way. "Ah, ye beggarly knave! Where did ye steal that cloak? Out with ye, or we'll rouse the Watch and throw ye in Bedlam with the madmen!"

Just at the door, Ben Jonson turned, took careful aim, and as both bricks sailed through the air, he flung himself at the dangling rope ladder and shook it hard.

A hurtling body fell at his feet, and he leaped upon it with knees, fists and teeth. Screams of rage and pain rose in the dusty arena as all the workmen swarmed down from galleries and penthouse to rescue their companion.

"Help! Murder! Send for the constable!"

"Death to ye all! Approach, ye beetle-headed, flap-eared, malmsey-nosed knaves! Ah, let me knock your hollow noggins until all bells ring!"

Bad enough for a starveling poet and ragged player to be so terrible a fighter, but the carpenters and plasterers knew nothing to do that would muffle his frightful roaring and howling. Blood streamed down the hollow cheeks of the marvellously cursing Jonson as he became more joyful with his war against all enemies he had ever known or heard of, and the hammer he had snatched from a carpenter was a fine weapon too, he found.

Shrewdly tucking his head in like a turtle, and rolling right away from the flailing and kicking carpenters out through the broad doorway, he went roaring, howling, laughing and still epically cursing all the way down Maid Lane to Deadman's Place, where he fetched up in a fruiterer's barrow.

The little old men of the Watch were hiding under a penthouse behind Old Man Sore's alehouse.

A rabble of whores, watermen, pirates, sailors, coney-catchers, and the ever-coursing thieves was streaming into Mr. Francis Langley's new Swan.

"A good time to leave these precincts," said Ben Jonson, sitting up among a rather good display of apples.

"You'll pay for my fruit!" screamed an old fat apple-woman, making for the rapidly retreating young poet, into whose splendid pockets a number of ruddy-cheeked apples went.

"Later, mother!" he called back over his shoulder. "I'll make thee live forever, in all thy lard too!"

And all bloody as he was, and even more muddy, torn, ragged and filthy than before, he filtered like fading sunlight down alleys and behind barns until he reached Paris Garden Stairs, and here he stooped over the dark water until he could wash off his face in the Thames.

"Buy my apples, buy my apples, three for a penny!" he chanted, and in a little while had his fare across the river on a wherry.

"Well, ye ragged rogue, will ye come aboard for Cole Harbour or drown thyself?" snarled the old waterman, whose two lubberly boys stood ready with their long oars. The tide was running in fast from the Isle of Dogs, and the reek of slaughterhouses and glue factories came heavy from the east. Ben Jonson looked back once more to the huge rearing shape of the Swan and heard the hammers going again.

Some day I shall return here, to laugh at these scurvy fools who scorn me now.

"I'm for Fishmongers' Hall Stairs," he muttered, stepping down into the wherry and holding his long cloak away from the passengers, who were apprentices, porters, two leering grocers' boys, and two whores to match, if they could make one.

Disdaining to notice any of these people or to hear any of their rude comments on his astonishing appearance, he went and sat at the bow. Out of his poetical pocket he took the *Poetics* of Scaliger.

He turned to the weighty and immensely serious chapter

upon comedy, that earnest and solemn art which, according to Cicero, must ever be a copy of life, a mirror of custom, a representation of truth.

"All must have decorum," said the weighty Scaliger, "whether they be old men or slaves, warriors, lovers, pedants, even braggarts. All must to their own type be true, from whence it follows, as the night the day, that they can not then be false to the classic pattern of comedy, which, patterned after real life, must teach us wherein our inconsistencies and precious vices make us inconstant to that constant purpose of all creation, which is to win our minds from wickedness to virtue."

Ben grunted with satisfaction, and with scorn for these modern small-witted men like Shakespeare who knew nothing of classic decorum and order, with the result that their clowns, zanies, boobies, fools, brought forth a hodgepodge of unsuitable sentiments, observations, jests, old saws, legends, until you might call them monsters of ignorance, ragbags of conceited sayings and careless fancy, like everything in this laughable Shakespeare's repertory.

Laughable, ha ha!

But I will be firm, I will be level, I will be honest with him and his fellows, as I am with all men and to a certain degree with women. It is my duty to teach them. It is my destiny to reform the corrupted drama of these degraded times. It is my mission to be the saviour of the English stage. Ages yet to come will bless my name for what I do.

What was that snickering from the grocers' boys? At whom were the wenches nodding, while they whispered and nudged one other?

A sudden cold wind whipped up the water through the arches of the great bridge, and its mighty shadow darkened all breathing human creatures on that small bobbing shell as the two lubberly boys toiled at the oars. The scream of gulls came raw and hungry on that wind, as from the great restless sea that was their mother. Ben Jonson shivered, and drew his cloak about him. High up there against the dirty sky he counted twelve, thirteen, fourteen heads of traitors, priests, conjurers, traders with Satan or the King of Spain.

I never liked how the ravens knock at their brainpans quite so loud, an they would wake them unto Judgment.

Alas, what is this our life, to be so soon waked from, but a little getting, spending, and making winter love in a dark corner?

chapter two

〰〰 THERE seemed to be some argument at Drinkwater Wharf, just above and beyond Old Swan Stairs. You could hear screams and yells coming up Crooked Lane all the way to the Black Bell Hostelry.

A large square-shouldered wench, working the pump at the Crest, tossed up her big wild head like a startled mare.

"That's my Ben," she said. "I know his noise anywhere."

"Oh Lord, mistress, what us poor vessels have to bear!" whimpered Goodie Lickepennie, wife of the old-clothes man of Candlewick Street Ward.

"A good month since the last time, God give me patience," said Ben Jonson's wife, an alehouse-keeper's daughter. "A bitter waste it is. Well, they can never say I took him for his money."

Running footsteps approached from Crooked Lane, and the neighbourhood dogs were pricking up their sharp ears and lifting their voices.

"Justice! Justice! In broad daylight!" some excited female was screaming from Bottle-Ale Way, toward the water.

And sure enough, the wild-haired wanderer arrived soon after.

He sidled up to the conduit of sweet water, famous of long-time among the whole uneasy brotherhood of stock fishmongers and salt-fishmongers, since they were inadvertently united in 1536, the 28th of Old Harry. He was hardly breathing above an ordinary deep wheeze and whistle, which was his wonted wind, and after splashing some of the sweet water over his face, neck and ears, and rinsing off his knobby paws, he heaved his awkward body round and grinned up into his wife's meaty face, with the two little cold boring blue eyes and the tart mouth as if she had recently spat out a mouthful of something gone bad.

"Well, dear one, how is it here?" he inquired, in a rusty voice enough to make you cover up your ears.

"Where's the money?" she snapped.

He wiped off his dripping head and hands on her apron and tossed it over her face.

"Ah, you she-bear! Is this a greeting?"

"Hang thee for a barber-surgeon's skellikin! Famine is in thy cheeks, hell in thy breath, a bonfire in thy belly, and an old broken tobacco-pipe in thy throat. Tell me, friends, is this a husband, with but half a face tied to an old bag of bones?"

"For God's sake, wife, let us be private about these matters," Ben muttered, as quite a good crowd of fishwives from Billingsgate Ward, Bridge Ward Within, and Candlewick Street Ward began to gather to see the show. Until the daily market opened here in Old Stocks Hall, they were free and ready for anything good to fribble away the time.

"Good day, Mrs. Lickepennie dear, I have business with your goodman husband," Ben said smoothly, if the grating of his scrannel-pipes could ever be called so.

"Oh, my suffering trunk and tripes!" remarked his wife, her salty speech revealing her origin in that teeming ward above river-water's ebb, where population was plentiful and citizens were sharp. "Shall I have patience to endure this broken brand of life? Was this the fortune I was born for? Walking ague, black jaundice and the gut-gripe take thee, ere thou pick my placket again."

"Well, ladies, I'll see you later," said the weary and shrunken wanderer, looking so pale, withered, starved and dried out that it was a wonder he could stagger a little way farther on his short bandy legs, in their baggy nether-stocks full of holes. Bowing all round to the grinning fishwives of three parishes, the subdued husband took up his wife's water pitcher, a huge vessel holding three gallons, and went along quite obediently behind her toward the Black Bell Hostelry, where her mean old father let her live and serve the carters and horse-coursers for her food and a corner.

Pray God I may crawl in a corner too, until I have bartered my brains for a new wardrobe, the exhausted prodigal prayed to any deity who was listening, whether of the Catholics, the Presbyterians, or the Water-Baptists.

Unfortunately an argument developed at the Black Bell Hostelry shortly before supper, between Cuthbert Buckle, a carter, Andy Bokerel, a pepperer, Roger Bongey, a skinner, Benjamin Jonson, who said he was a poet, and Mrs. Benjamin Jonson, the host's daughter.

There was much throwing about of brains, later of pint pots, quart pots, pickle pots, chamber pots, and tosspots, with the result that the calm, reasonable and rational Mr. Jonson continued the discussion in Finke's Lane with the nine or fifteen potmen, foysters, tanners, fruiterers, three meal-weighers, one yeoman of the wood wharfs, a carver's man and a water bailiff who now seemed to be his principal enemies and antagonists in that quarter.

When Finke's Lane became crowded the twenty-seven or so battlers adjourned in the direction of the great brewhouse at Puddle Wharf, somehow managing to deprive themselves of the company of that plentiful apostrophizer and explainer who still commanded all words in the world but was persuaded to abandon the field to all ranters, utterers, stutterers and futterers who cared to occupy it.

Being tired at that time, the disappearing poet decided to find a place to rest somewhere between the pillory on Cornhill, which might be occupied, the porch of Allhallows Grasse Church in Lombard Street, and the friendly shelter of Pickthatch Close, where the brotherhood of thieves lived.

Alas, that a man like me should be so reduced! My tricks exceed my stitches. Oh, I am out of clutch!

Well, it takes a knack to save a knave, and my last word to the jealous is, let 'em fear.

But as he plodded on through crooked alleys and down mean ways, he shed a tear or two for poor Anne, his wife, already cold in bed while that virile youth, her husband, must tool up his wits and find himself another corner.

So he came at last to that meanest of churches in all Billingsgate Ward, poor old bare St. Buttolph's, overwhelmed by strangers and greedy men of spoil. No door to keep out the wanderer, no watchman or sexton to mind the vessels and the monuments; no vessels and no monuments. All had been torn out, pulled down, defaced, carried off by the plunderers of the glorious Reformation in King Harry's time. Here in these sordid alleys where the rats now ran, the pious nuns had once chanted sweet canticles of devotion to their prince of the peaceful heart.

Ah God, perhaps my shrew is right, the weary wanderer thought. For secretly she is a Catholic and yearns for holiness, especially in me.

Well, I'm not dying yet. Enough time to confess my sins later.

And bestowing his old coachman's cloak about him as comfortably as he could in rats' alley behind a desecrated tomb, he laid him down to sleep, lulled by the scamperings and squeakings of the merry rats, who would inherit the earth.

He was soon smacking his lips over his dreams. The world was good to eat, a great pompion riding in the sky, beneath a moon that was a silver potato. Aha, a fat partridge next his pillow. Buttered shrimps borne by his loving shrew, now slim and smiling, ready to kiss him like a scallop, close, and tickle him with her mother tongue.

Someone woke him, feeling in his pockets, and he sprang right up out of sleep howling.

Whoever it was scuttered off along the spoiled alleys of the degraded church.

Ben Jonson yawned and stretched, and began to tiptoe through the glimmering and uncertain darkness.

Where the altar once had been he saw two thieves crouched over a heap of spoil, and felt his ears move with excitement.

Ah, not for nothing have I known the base Egyptians of the dark mountains of Darby.

He crept closer, closer, feeling in his most secret pocket for that most precious pot of goose grease tinctured with phosphorus, much employed by the Abram men to frighten housewives in the country.

"This one is mine, ye dog," one thief was saying.

"Lay by, or I'll snick thy snaff," answered his fellow.

But then there arose between them a spectral figure, as from a desecrated tomb, moaning horribly in Greek, its ghastly countenance shining like a dead mackerel in the moonlight, which there was none of in here.

The thieves departed with their sins upon them, leaving their loot behind.

Some little time after that a long, lean shadow departed also from that church, bearing the shadow of a bundle on its back.

The shadow melted into the shadows of the deep, dark, mild, moony night, headed for Bosse Alley toward that spring of ever-running water which stood by Billingsgate and had been made to run in memory of Dick Whittington.

For in putting on new garments it was well to bathe in clean water, for the good of the soul, the body and the garments.

So it had been a good day after all.

chapter three

WHO was this handsome young man in the feathered hat and the stuffed breeches?

How kingly was his bearing! How intelligent his countenance!

"By God, boys, it's Jonson in some handed-down glory-clothes! Run for your lives!"

Dick Burbage speaking sideways into the astonished faces of his fellows as they smoked and laughed in Curtain Close. It was ten o'clock on a Tuesday morning, and they had assembled for the rehearsal of a comedy that was still a good get-penny in the provinces.

That old wedding-piece their Shakespeare had written and rewritten for three marriages already, and was patching up again for his rich patron's mother — *A Midsummer Night's Dream.*

Bowing politely to a few loitering ladies, and lifting his Spanish felt a good English foot from the top of his head, Mr. Benjamin Jonson bore down upon the players of the Queen's cousin, Henry Carey, Lord Hunsdon, who was now her Lord Chamberlain, but was lying sick at home of a feverish flux.

"Good day, sweet ladies, have ye seen Mr. Shakespeare today?"

"Not yet, sir, and how we do love the dear kind gentleman!"

"Well, he will be along soon, belike," Mr. Jonson told the poor simple creatures. "For any player is fined a day's pay if he is late for rehearsal."

"Oh, but sweet Mr. Shakespeare is a poet, and above mere playing!" a big-eyed piece of frailty informed him.

"I keep his *Venus and Adonis* under my pillow!" said a wench with a face like a dish, and nothing any good in it.

Patience, patience, said Ben to himself, approaching the stage door of the Curtain playhouse, which stood in Curtain Close. How swiftly all the players had hurried inside!

Was it raining? No, the day was dull and dim, but not dropping yet.

Shall I stay and confront their Shakescene as he comes, smiling to these giddy fools who know no better than to love him? No, it is the better part of wisdom to go *sub silentio*. And I may see how he puts them through their limps and stumbles, and have the jump on him from the start.

Strange! They had locked the door after them!

What could they fear in Shoreditch, in this Liberty of Holywell, where the creeping justices of London had no power?

He gave the door a delicate salute with a mere teasing of knuckles — the knock courteous.

I will be calm. Patience becomes me, and I it.

No answer to the knock courteous.

A man like me, the which there is none under heaven, is not put down by these slight men.

And he gave the panel the smart yet dainty tap known as the knock modest.

Let them hear, if they have ears.

Hark! Was that a snort of smothered mirth?

Hang 'em, the slaves! Shall my rage not rise and smite 'em where they stand?

Calm, calm. Their Shakescene is not yet come. He is my meat, not they.

I now bestow upon these shadows of no substance such a knock as will ring their bells from binnacle to galley-west and back.

And raising his great knobby fist he dealt the poor cracked panel such a blow that a few dull loiterers about the archery-butts came strolling over to see and hear what might be another summons to justice, or writ of misfeasance, or search

and seizure, of which there were many against such mis-
fortune's men as these.

Ben Jonson backed up like a billy goat and hurled himself
forward. At that moment the door suddenly opened and he
was precipitated inside.

Howling with righteous rage and braying out curses enough
to blister all whoreson upright rabbits in the whole scurvy
company, he clattered all the way across the tiring room,
through the red and yellow striped curtains of the inner stage,
and into a frail fabrication of sticks and canvas, painted and
bestuck with gewgaws, representing Titania's bower. Down
came the bower all over him in a cloud of dust and plaster,
together with an ass-head of papier-mâché a little too big for
him, so that it quite covered his angry screaming head and
muffled his message, which was still being delivered from
within the enormous jaws of his supplementary head while
laughter from all the players continued.

A stately handsome man, who had just come strolling into
the playhouse to the enthusiastic greetings of all the females
waiting to catch a glimpse of him, now held up his hand and
silenced the happy players.

"A good entrance," said Shakespeare. "A very good entrance, the whiff and wind of whose passage will so unnerve
the house it will be senseless, and as hush as death."

Ben Jonson, sprawling in the ruins of Titania's bower, was
pulling at the ass-head with both hands while his legs kicked
at anything that moved.

"Methinks he did enter with a bridegroom's fresh alacrity,
yet he fell something short on performance," Shakespeare
added, but laughter drowned his words.

Now from the ruins arose the fallen scholar, hooting within
his ominous ass-head and still afflicted with it as he staggered
and stumbled about, fighting for freedom and fresh air.

"Ah, I've never seen him look better," said old Heminge,
the grave man of the company.

"It is true he is translated, but into a better species," said

Henry Condell. "Willy, let us hire him to make more en-trances."

"Shall we not have him go out and come in again, that we may see the full classical majesty of his coming?" asked Burbage.

But the pale pockmarked face of Ben Jonson, sprinkled with plaster-dust, crowned with red hair as wild as the snakes of Medusa, now shot forth out of its prison, and his indignant voice with it.

"Ah, you scurvy-valiant asses!" he howled, throwing the cracked ass-head at the gleeful players. "Oh, you strutting sacks of guts and sin, with no more brain in your heads than I have in my elbows, the world is pestered with your prating plays! Your wit was mouldy when your grandsires hung from trees!"

His harsh voice howled from the rafters of the Curtain as whickering laughter rose around him.

He turned toward the stately master of this company, that smooth man of country wit who had flattered his way into eminence while better poets grovelled and starved — Shake-speare the ladies' please-man, glossy with popularity, easy liv-ing, good food and his own high opinion. Ah, look at him there, so gracefully poised that he might be a court gallant at a tilting, protected by the powerful, honoured by the Queen, well-larded by success and fatuous with plenty!

"And you, sir, you, sir, I say you, sir, I say damn all your plays, damn them, sir!"

His voice broke and he began to sob, putting his hands to his haggard cheeks.

"Why, we were but having a foolish jest or so," Shakespeare began, in that voice with such harmony in it that people stopped their noise to listen. "Stay and laugh with us, good friend, do . . ."

But the weeping Jonson, muttering to himself because he could no longer speak without shame, went staggering out of the playhouse and off into the common fields, pulling at his ragged hair and his stolen clothes, as if he would pluck himself bald and naked before his inglorious exit was ended.

They looked out from the Curtain and saw him stamping and shaking his fists at trees and windmills, until the mist mercifully covered him.

chapter four

❦❦❦ THE swooning weather blew away in a big blast from Boreas, and all England huddled and shivered under the nipping fingers of the frost. Who saw Ben Jonson in his new suit? Who cared?

Who heard him in the howling wind? Who knew where he had gone now?

Old James Burbage, disappointed in the English weather again, closed up his two leaky old playhouses in Shoreditch and spent all the money he had on renovating the old Revels storehouse in Blackfriars to make a fashionable new theatre there.

"Pray God we will not be haunted by the ghosts of the friars," Shakespeare said. He always thought of ghosts in old buildings. If there were none there he dreamed new ones.

Neither in Curtain Close, nor the Liberty of Paris Garden, nor even in the Red Bull or any other common place for players, did the Lord Chamberlain's Men gather to rehearse their shows that winter. And so they forgot about Ben Jonson until the morning they saw him briefly at the Falcon Tavern in Southwark, where old Henslowe was scolding his play-cobblers for the bad condition of his coffers.

Rattling up pots and pans in the scullery, the classical scholar in the stolen clothes came tiptoeing out every few minutes to peek at the players and mutter curses in Latin.

"Ah, I did well to leave them all," he said, sidling closer to the padded bench where old Henslowe lolled, with eager flatterers on both sides of him.

One of the Chamberlain's Men, old Austin Phillips, overheard his mutter and whispered something to Henry Condell.

Ben Jonson eyed them suspiciously. What were they saying about him? Why was it that little men of no good repute and

35

less wit always disclosed their envy of those rare men who were better endowed?

Meanwhile the rival Admiral's Men clustered close around the moneylender, pawnbroker and whoremaster, also church-warden. But the old man had a sharp eye, and saw Ben skulking near.

"Hey there, bricklayer!" he cackled. "Where are the two acts I paid you for? Must I send the beadle round to Pick-thatch Close for my property? Come closer, come closer," he added, peering suspiciously at Ben's new suit. "Who gave ye those clothes? They look like some odd ones I had from my Lord's last inventory of dead men's stuff."

Ben answered with saintly patience, meanwhile going away: "Sir, your slight play will be in your hands next week without fail. It is family reasons. My wife. Our infant girl — our little Mary —" Was the scarecrow crying?

"See that ye are not wanting, or I'll have ye by the heels into the Clink again!" old Henslowe screeched after the re-treating starveling. He really looked frightful this winter. Could any man shrink farther into his essential skeletal stuff than this, without being it?

"Oons, they should feed the poor scrag," Henslowe said kindly to Gabriel Spencer, his most trusted player.

"He is bottomless, I know for a fact," Spencer said, shrug-ging his fat shoulders.

And they went on with their discussion of what old plays they would cobble up to last out the season, or such rags of it as were left by the wintry winds.

Only Shakespeare, who often wandered away from the sweaty taverns and the stinking smoke to be alone with his thoughts, happened to see the classical scholar skulking about the alleys of Shoreditch a little later that morning.

I must contrive to ease him out of Fortune's scullery and into the eye of favour, the thoughtful poet decided. No man should eat himself with such misery as this. But how? He carries his doom right with him, like a candle-snuffer.

It was on the way down Maiden Lane, and Jonson could not avoid him without turning tail and running.

"Good morrow, Mr. Jonson. Have you heard Gabriel Spencer is forming his own company?"

His bright and cheerful voice was just the wrong sound for shivering Jonson, cursing his own darkness.

Ha! The man who mocked me before them all.

"Hang him!" said Ben, his face so deadly pale already it could turn no more, unless to corpse-grey. "I'll split him and truss him up like a rabbit-sucker. Ah, that small fetid carnivorous weasel! That underfed shrew! May he and all players henceforth avoid me, or I'll brain their small remnant of mind-stuff with a thimble!"

"A neat trick if 'twere done when it is done, though God forbid it should be done," Shakespeare said, as he deftly slipped a shilling into the horrible old cloak that still could not get the starveling warm.

"Good day to you, sir!" snarled Ben, while down his nose dripped something like a tear, or the salt-rheum perhaps.

"Good day, Mr. Jonson, and we hope to see you on our stage again," Shakespeare remarked pleasantly, stepping out smartly toward the Liberty of Paris Garden, where the bear-baitings still went on anyhow, no matter how ill the weather.

"Ha!"

What a world of scorn in that little sound!

I hate thee, Shakespeare, his private voice continued. Oh, misery and injustice of this wicked world, that a man like me must fawn and cringe before a witless countryman like thee!

I hear he sent his wife and three children back to Stratford again. The better to consort with his rich friends and low wenches. The man is bloody, bad, and ungrammatical. I can prove it by twenty references to his scurvy history plays. History! Are they history? Murder and uproar, villains and stranglers, killers of little princes! Our own Francis Bacon has proved that Richard never did it! I am astonished that her Majesty allows it. *He* hopes to see me on his stage again! *Our* stage, he says! Who says it is his, or theirs? Besides, there is too much lechery in his plays. Look at his poems. Immoral clean through, while snivelling and sermonizing about the very sins he holds up to shameful view. And those damned sonnets he slips into his friends' pockets — flat buggery I say, with his grovelling adoration of this pretty lad and that rich lord, while his own poor wife and three children go ragged and starve in Stratford. Oh, he stinks to heaven, this totter-up of profits in the play business, while better men . . . while men much better . . . while a man like me . . .

His angry, rolling eye, swivelling up and down Love Lane, where a dozen bawdy houses were, had just picked out Shakespeare strutting by the House of the Three Luces, where many lousy lechers were wont to roll in sin.

Look at him there! In full light of day too! Has the man no churchly decency? Can he not wait till evening for his dark and lustful assignations?

However, Shakespeare went past the Three Luces and straight on, bowing politely in that maddening way of his to all such frail females as cast their eyes upon him; and tiptoeing after him now came Conscience in a ragged cloak, or to put it frankly, Ben Jonson, muttering all the way.

No ladies spoke to him, no matter how hotly he glared at them. Of course none of them knew about his new suit and his stuffed breeches. A dank and dowly day, and a man so empty must wrap his cloak around him.

Oh God, to tell me that Gabriel Spencer has been chosen to head a company, while I . . . while I . . . with my learning, with my knowledge, with my genius, with my . . .

His clawing fingers, searching for some classical comfort in his literary pocket, touched a coin.

A coin!

Could I have missed it before?

How could I have missed it?

Merciful providence, hast thou at length started to breed silver in my pocket?

He trembled and crossed himself, although not believing,

of course. As he brought out the new bright Liza shilling from the poetical pocket, his rolling eye lit on the man of his wrath marching straight up to the gloomy gate of the Marshalsea Prison.

Oh God!

A wave of nausea rose within the starveling poet. Only by the charity of a missionary priest did I escape that house of horror, pain and death. Why should he, who was going to die, have blessed me and slipped me a sh . . . .

Fire and balls!

A shilling! A shilling! A pretty new shilling!

His shaking fingers, unaccustomed to such wealth, dropped the shining coin upon the muddy ground. He stooped and got it before any idler snatched it from him.

And then the shameful truth hit him like a cowflap in the chops.

Toads and vipers!

I am insulted.

Bugs and tortures!

I'll not endure it. No, no, I'll fling it at his mincing feet, and be damned to him for a hypocritical snob.

Here I go, to fling his shilling at Shakescene the cheapener of worth he could never buy.

Ben Jonson bit the coin, smelt it, felt it, and wrapped it quickly in a dirty handkerchief.

He glared at the hideous prison into which the lucky countryman had vanished.

Hark! Was that some poor starving prisoner, giving his last groan before dying?

His stomach gave a sickening heave.

Oh God, that cruelty grows fat, while good men shrink and shrivel! Bad times, bad times, poor England!

Last time they clapped me in the Clink, I would have died of hunger if that sweet little woman had not found me in my despair of God, whispered a prayer in Latin, and given me bread and wine.

Poor frail creature, with her great gentle eyes!

Mistress Martha they call her, but that's only her name to the priest-hunters. I think her name is Lynn, Ann Lynn.

A woman of breeding and wealth, they say, from Ringwood in Hampshire, now widowed. They killed her husband last year.

Pray God they have not hunted her down, for I do believe she shelters missionary priests in her house.

Many an implausible squire have I observed coming out of it, and they go disguised in that condition.

Ben sighed over the poor condition of Christianity too, that always now must be rending its own, and making more martyrs than ever the Romans did.

But futile regret always made him hungry, and he was so starved now that he had better spend the shilling on food at the Falcon.

Who knows? Gabriel might blow a good part my way, or he might need a new comedy of humours.

Just then a shuttered black coach stopped at the back door of the Marshalsea and two pursuivants went sneaking in.

Mercy of God! I thought the evil man was far away in the North, stretching poor gipsies on the rack!

Ben trembled at the sight of the Queen's torturer, that authorized tormenter who boasted of having a machine at home that made the common rack seem child's play — Richard Topcliffe, the cruellest tyrant of all England, a man most infamous and hateful to all the realm for his bloody and butcherly mind.

For one evil instant Ben caught the gloating glare of those feverish red-rimmed eyes as the greedy old man strode into the hideous prison. Lean, vigorous, ravenous as a wolf, already grinning at the delicious prospect.

Ben Jonson trembled and felt cold.

Suppose Shakescene is on some business for his Catholic friends! There is whispering too that he is not as devout as he looks in church, and may even look kindly on atheists, Jews, blackamoors and gipsies.

But how could he be a non-believer, and drool out such pious sayings in his plays?

And though he had a cousin who lost his head for being a papist, surely this Shakescene loves money too much to pay the fine of a recusant.

No, it's impossible.

He's visiting some blackamoor in chains. Or a madman, to hear from his gibbering lips the fool's phrases for his next vulgar comedy.

Or perchance he is tiring of Black Luce of Clerkenwell, his favourite whore.

I'm clear, I'm free.

I'll go spend it. I'll spend it, I will squander it, nothing can stop me from feeding myself on it.

One, two, here I go.

Indeed he took four halting steps toward the Falcon Tavern. Then as if great hands seized him and turned him round, he started toward the prison on the run.

chapter five

〰〰 SO quickly did the pursuivants drag out their victim that the few moans and cries, the words of justice muttered, and the scuffling and thumping as they pulled and shoved him into the coach with the iron shutters, were soon over, and the hungry-eyed Ben barely noticed this small happening. It was crowded, noisy, squalid and filthy in the common grovelling place where pickpockets, whores, murderers, night-wanderers all squirmed, fought, quarrelled and snarled together.

But where was Shakescene?

Ben found him in earnest conversation with a gross bailiff, and he saw him slip the sordid lout a gold coin.

H'm, this man has more in him than I thought.

Pray God he is not aiding papistical priests, or he cannot last. This is no age for pity or looking backward. Onward! To the gallows!

Just then somebody stumbled into him, giving him a shrewd dig with an elbow. Ben opened his mouth to utter a classical curse, and saw it was the famous playwright's little brother, the wild and dissolute Ned, who played princesses and milkmaids for the Chamberlain's Company.

Drunk again. Now he reeled right into the arms of the great Shakescene, and Ben heard that famous voice raised in stern reproach.

"Thou sodden lump of pale superfluity, behold thy fate!"

Ben hugged himself. Shakescene the Great was pointing to a ragged sot who lay sprawled in his own vomit.

Ah, ah, so this is the gentle Shakespeare playing a scene of domestic life.

How wrong his feeling is for words, how lame are his moral observations!

Meanwhile the muttering, cursing boy, his long hair tumbling over his face, fell from his brother's arms and sprawled beside a little frail woman who was lying ill on some rags.

A shudder went through Ben Jonson. Mercy of God, have they got her in their claws?

The holy woman who had visited him in this very prison, and given him bread and wine.

Ben came trembling closer. "Alas, Mrs. Lynn, to see you here!" he whispered.

Why was Shakespeare eyeing him so sternly? The frail woman gave the trembling scholar a luminous smile and blessed him with her eyes.

"Come, lend me a hand with this sponge of mine," Shakespeare murmured.

Ben sighed heavily and could think of no help he could give the holy woman but to bestow his shilling upon her, which he did, putting it into her hand as frail as a bird's claw, and patting it. "Give me half of the boy," he said.

Young Ned was astonishingly awkward for one so animated by grace on the stage. How well he played the laughing, witty wenches that were the glory of Shakescene's comedies!

Ay, the man knows women through and through, I'll give him that, Ben thought. Young Ned was a thin, pale, tall boy, with glossy black hair that curled like a Welshman's.

Astonishing, too, the strength with which he pulled Ben Jonson away from poor Mrs. Lynn.

"I'm sorry for that poor soul there," Ben muttered as he helped Shakespeare get his brother to the iron gate.

Shakespeare paid no attention to these Christian sentiments. Another aspect of his character — cold, cold, unless there was money to be made.

"Well, boys will do it, from time to time," said the gross turnkey at the gate, grinning with all fangs bared as he allowed them to go through.

"Ah, they will," said Shakespeare.

And they were out, but Ben still worried over Mrs. Lynn. What if the torturer Topcliffe had found her out? I'll go back later, he thought. Say nothing to point the finger at me. But meanwhile, lead him on to some disclosure if I can.

"All families have some weak limb or branch," he began. "Horace declares the truth of it, and Scaliger supports him."

Shakespeare appeared edified at this classical information, but Ned drooled, spat and cursed as they bundled him along down Dead Man's Lane.

"*Sunt delicta tamen quibus ignovisse velimus,*" Ben said, quoting from good old Horace.

Shakespeare looked vague.

I have heard the man was for a while a schoolmaster in the country, Ben thought. Ha, I will try him, and if I trap him, *spes sibi quisque, stemmata quid faciunt?*

But while they meandered and plunged, stopped and started, and plunged on again with the vigorously drunken brother, quite a large crowd of low and evil persons came snickering, sneering, giggling and guffawing after them.

"Βράχεια τερψις ἐστίν ἡδονης κακης," Ben said, thinking he would try a little Greek. If he has small Latin, this Shakespeare has less Greek, that is sure.

"Μη κρινετε ἱνα μη κριθητε," Shakespeare answered, to the classical scholar's disgust. He was just about to smother him with great Greek wisdom, when the gibes and jeers of the crowd pretty much made it necessary to get the boy on board a wherry and depart from here.

They slipped and stumbled down Paris Garden Stairs just in time to reach a boat now bobbing there on the oily tide. Poor Ned seemed almost gone, muttering groans and curses and sliding over the stones of the pier, almost upsetting Ben Jonson and his brother together.

Blast the boy's eyeballs! He was blaspheming in Latin.

Am I being made mock of? Is that possible? Ben thought. He was still considering the most dignified, the most stately, the most unutterably awful punishment for such discourtesy when they stumbled and plunged aboard, almost upsetting the wherry and its passengers before they had Ned stowed swooning in the stern.

"Oh, what a sorry sight!" said a fat lady at the bow.

"Boys is all going to the dogs, these days," said a fishmonger.

"What's the world coming to?" a brewer wanted to know.

"You may well ask, master," said a leather-seller.

I'll leave 'em to lurch as they may, Ben decided, and with his face in the air, as though looking for a friend among the birds, he started for the stairs. Ned sprawled and flung out a leg, the wherry drew sharply away from the slippery stones, the brawny oarsmen pushed off and dug in their long oars, and the scholarly Scot lay upended in the bilge-water at the bow. Loud cheers came to his ears from the boobies on Paris Garden Stairs, mingled with hoots and whistles.

So they departed from the Bankside in Southwark, and Ben spoke no more Latin or Greek all the way to Blackfriars Stairs, across the river.

I'll let him have the full blast of my displeasure, Ben decided, when he was right side up and glowering at Shakespeare. Damn the man, he was smiling kindly, and holding the worthless boy's head in his lap.

"Sir, sir, I'll say to you now, sir —" Ben began, but Shakespeare just put his finger to his lips and asked him to supper. What? What?

"Do come and have supper with us, Mr. Jonson. Tom Pope sets a good table, and I would ask your advice on a history we might do next."

"Sir, sir, I am not sure I have the time," Ben stammered, while he felt the saliva starting up. Supper! At Tom Pope's! The fattest man in the company, and a great drinker too.

"If you are at liberty this week, there is a part to play as a hired man in something we're about to do," that ineffable Shakescene added.

Ben ran out of English, and could only move his jaws open and shut. His throat went dry, his stomach jumped, and he clamped his teeth together just in time.

"I will think about it," he finally mumbled.

"Do that," said Shakespeare, beaming upon him as if he loved him like a brother.

A brother! Pah!

The watermen rowed well away from the currents of the bridge, or the wherry would have been drawn into the rapids and whirled around.

God save us from a fish dinner, Ben prayed, and did his best to seem friendly. A whole flock of beautiful white swans glided and bobbed past them, but their limber necks made the starving scholar feel dizzy.

"You are kind to your brother," he croaked.

"My mother put me in charge of poor Ned from the first time he held breath, turned black in the face, and would not live."

"What did you do?"

"Made faces at him till he laughed, and lived."

"Ah, it is a good way," said Ben.

A sudden chilly breeze swept up the river from the east.

Now we've had so mild a winter, no doubt we'll have the shivering spring for which poor England is famous, he thought.

Looming ever nearer now, just beyond Bridewell, they saw the broad stairs of Blackfriars, and the gatehouse.

"Burbage has spent seven hundred pound on our new playhouse quarters in Blackfriars," Shakespeare said, his gentle countenance full of pain at so much money spent on anything. People said the man was a miser, would not be debauched, and when invited to, wrote that he was in pain.

In pain where? In pain how?

In the purse, I think, Ben Jonson decided, watching the smooth and ruddy face of this successful poet. The very terms are cancellations of each other, by God! How can a poet ever be rich? This man is a fraud. If he were not so damnably modest, meek and mild, so sweet in temper, so full of grace he is like some Sister of Charity over a shriven sinner, I swear by Beelzebub I would hate him, I would, yes I would.

It was not nearly such a struggle getting the drunken brother out of the wherry and up the slimy stairs. Strange! The closer they came to the gatehouse the straighter Ned stood, the better he walked, the stronger he got. So that by the time they were nodding to the gatekeeper and passing under the arch into the handsome enclosure in which only lords, gentlemen and rich shopkeepers lived, young Ned was able to stand up and laugh at them. And then he kissed his famous brother on both cheeks, slapped Ben Jonson's chest and shoulders, and began to dance around them both like some Robin Goodfellow out of the mad woods of fancy.

"Pox! We've been gulled all the way!" Ben groaned, near collapse.

"Oh, thou wert ever so full of sympathy as an old woman! Oh, oh, the sourest man in England, and I had thee weeping for sweet pity!" Ned cried, and choked.

"Silence!" said Shakespeare. The boy shut up at once.

Hardly in time. Two glum-looking constables plodded toward them out of Water Lane, marching a perennial drunkard ahead of them, little old Tom Box, the tinker.

"Good morrow, my good friends," said Shakespeare to them, as if he were lord of the manor.

"Good day to you, Master Shackspurr, sir, and you too, Master Ned," said the constables, knuckling at their hats. "And from me too, to you two," mumbled Tom Box.

But they eyed the stranger in the long ragged cloak pretty hard. And old Tinker Tom cried out, "That fellow's a drinker, a picker and a stealer, and not to be trusted!"

"Get along there, Tom," said the constables.

"Now by all the proctors of the Court of Arches, I'd swear out an action against you both for cozening rogues," said Ben, leaning with his last gasp against a handsome porch, belonging to Lord Cobham, who hated players like the pox.

Shakespeare put his finger to his lips and shook his head.

Ben snorted and choked awhile, bottling his wretched temper. It was still not supper time by a whole half day, unless they supped at noon.

"Could we make it dinner, and now?" he whispered, ready to give in for good.

"Take him under the left wing, Neddie," Shakespeare said, just before the surly starveling collapsed on the pavement.

And so together, the two brothers supported their new companion all the way into the Purple Pig, a very good modest tavern of that quarter.

"Explain me this, ex-ex-explain it," yattered Ben Jonson as they set him down on a red leather padded bench.

"After thou hast had beer and food, where there are no ears but ours," Shakespeare promised, beaming at the abused, confused, and bemused young cynic with the classical education. And he beckoned to a pretty barmaid with a darling pair bobbing in full view, and two of the merriest eyes above them that the starving bad actor had ever seen. He gave a great sigh, and fainted with happiness.

chapter six

⚜⚜ SO it was that the Lord Chamberlain's Men acquired another player, for as long as the city fathers allowed them to play that memorable year. But so fuddled with unaccustomed warmth, wine, friendship and food did Ben become that gaudy night, so amorous with the wench, so wordy with the swarm of listening ears attached, he thought, to gentlemen's and players' heads, that he never remembered on what mission it was that naughty Ned had played his drunken part.

Better to know all, or know nothing, Ben decided, after he was sober.

Then too, these pestilential and picking rehearsals every day! A hard thing to keep his bargain, and the men of Lord Hunsdon's company played everything to the life of plain old English day, instead of strutting and spouting, as old Henslowe's players did.

"It is not so in Seneca, it was never so in Aristotle's *Poetics*, and neither the Italians, the French, nor the great Greeks would countenance such undertoning and wishy-washing," he informed the patient Shakespeare.

"It may be so, Ben, it might be so again, and indeed it once was so, but I've never liked it," said the gentle Shakespeare.

Oh, the yawning mornings in the newly renovated rooms of the old Blackfriars dining hall, stumbling over his big tired feet while he tried to be a good and dutiful murderer as the kindly man of Stratford instructed!

"I've always torn it and strutted it afore," Ben grumbled. "Alleyn and Gabriel both taught me so. And my master Aristotle —"

The carpenters and plasterers were roosting all over the new beams and scantlings of the Burbages' costly new playing-rooms. For the lords and gentles and their highflown ladies, this was to be — no more splitting the ears of the groundlings, as Shakespeare called the outmoded ranting ways of the Admiral's Men.

49

Ben began to hear the whispers of mockers above and beyond him. Fops of the town and law-courts liked to attend rehearsals, and Shakespeare's fellows tolerated their giggles and quips right during the action.

Then too, the plasterers sometimes vouchsafed remarks; the carpenters had their words for it; even a few loitering apprentices from the tire-makers' and button-makers' shops would duck in to listen while Dick Burbage tore off a good yardage of bardage, and whistle if they misliked any of it.

"Why, there's no harm in a little criticism while we work our scenes up," Tom Pope explained. He was the fat man of the company, and Shakespeare and the naughty Ned shared his house with him and a few adopted children, not to speak of old Tom's two women, and such others as were meat for the Shakespeares. A scandal!

Just last month Shakespeare's poor Anne, strangely taken with melancholy and fits of gloom, had prevailed on him to ride her and the children back to Stratford.

No use for a poor countrywoman to endure the noise and swarming diseases of London, with a fine new house to be had in her native place. Or an old house new-built, whatever it was to be. One heard all kinds of sneers and gibes about Shakespeare's love-money from the giddy Southampton, whom he had flattered clear to his most secret pocketbook.

Well, if I could beg me a house from some silly lord, perhaps I might, Ben Jonson thought.

Though how I would afterwards go live in it with my poor shrew, or how the lustful Shakespeare will ever live in his with his, I cannot see.

"How is it with your wife?" Ben would ask, whenever he had the opportunity.

"She's better with her sisters in Shottery," the hypocrite answered, looking meek. "These cold winds, these fogs and smoky mists, and the plague that comes with flies in summer . . . ."

As if they had no flies in Stratford! Ah God!

Bear with me, ye stars of heaven! I hear his Anne caught

him in a cornfield, and would not let him up until he had paid his forfeit. A mere boy he was.

Well, they'll trap us.

"Places, gentlemen!" called old stuttering Heminge, who bustled about on company business while the Burbage brothers counted the money, Will Kempe horsed around to make the spectators laugh, the boys practised leaps and dodges, and the affable men of the company ran through some new lines they had written for Shakespeare to add to their parts.

"*We* never let any player add any idiocies to his own part!" snarled Ben. "This is wrong!"

"Well, it's all in play, Ben, all in play, and if we add 'em all in they may make a playwright," Shakespeare said, in that annoying way he had of burying at least one pun in every sentence.

"It is contrary to Aristotle, and against the Unities. The narrow humours of your players must not impose upon the central structure and total idea of your play."

"Well, well, we're mere common players, Ben, a loose fellowship of some rather good men, and when I find me a good old story to steal somewhere, if it has no fat part for Burbage, I write one in or let him help dress it up. The same for Phillips and Heminge and Pope, and Will Kempe always has to range as his wits will take him. Shall we take places, gentlemen? This morning we have three short scenes from our new *Romeo and Juliet* for her Majesty's Candlemas Revels. Johnny, you're the angry old father. Broad, absolute, you know, Johnny. Henry, you're the noble suitor Paris. Dick, you'll have to be sweet and gentle for Romeo. Ned, you're Juliet if your voice stays in the right register — but if not, there's a lively lad over at Chapel we can borrow. Nick, you be the nurse. Easy on the jests though. Let 'em drop like pearls, not crash like cannon balls."

"Who's to play Mercutio, Willy?" asked Dick Burbage, a sturdy, vigorous, masterful young owner of at least one playhouse and partner now in three.

"Well," Shakespeare said doubtfully, looking around. "H'm,

I see no one this morning quite moonstruck enough. I'll fill in until we try Mr. Jonson."

"For that pretty stuff?" Burbage said.

"No, no, for Tibalt, the prince of cats," Shakespeare said hastily. "He murders excellently, you know. He did Heironimo well."

"Romeo's a fool, I think," Burbage said.

"Well, it will be some variety for you then. Are we all assembled now? Mr. Jonson, downstage left, if you please. The rapiers and daggers, Nick. Tom, double as Capulet and the nurse for now. Henry, your first explosion is halfway down your part."

"I like not this letting of common players put in their own lines," Ben muttered to Ned. "The poet must be superior to all who merely speak."

"Ned, we need you to double as Benvolio," Shakespeare said.

"Gentlemen, I have a few thoughts before we begin," said Ben Jonson. "Let us consider if these fellows are Italians or Englishmen. Who can tell which from these lines full of country jests and imitation humours? What are we to make of this king of cats? There is no pun in the Italian. *Gatto,* it is, *gattone* if he is a large cat. Let us first of all renovate and revise him as Signior Gattone. We shall have laughter from scholars at once."

Dead silence from the company. Even the plasterers and carpenters stopped what they were doing. And two wags of the law-courts, young Marston and his current familiar, John Donne, looked as if they would split.

"Well, Ben, for an old tale that's been all around the barn and back again, perhaps we had best leave it as it is, and you can feed me some good lines for the next one," said the gentle Shakespeare.

"There is no constant humour of any kind in this play, old or new!" said Ben, heating up. "Your Romeo's a fool, raving over his black-eyed Rosalind one minute, then creeping into Juliet's bed the next."

"Good, that's the name for him. Dick, when the heavens fall on you, be sure you load that line with its full weight of woe: *O, I am Fortune's fool!*"

And he strolled downstage, nodding and waving to sundry shallow wits and idlers who might have money or influence, to try over some lines from the mad Mercutio's part, and see if he must cut them.

Ay, write himself the juiciest lines, whether the part calls for them or not, Ben thought. This is mere fooling.

Chatter and laughing stopped, and the haunted old frater where the Black Friars had dined and offered grace was now full of grace indeed.

"Oh socks, he kills me," muttered Robin Gough, the Welsh boy who played witty wenches and dull milkmaids, no matter what kind, until his voice was changed.

"He was better when he was young," Ned observed with narrowed eyes, waiting for his great brother to overreach himself. The time would come, perhaps.

The harmonious voice went on, like some golden viol of sense and spirit, played by a king of dreams, Queen Fancy's own musician.

"But this is all out of tune with the play! Not one single authority of antiquity would allow it!"

This from Ben Jonson, his hair wilder, his face paler, his shanks thinner than ever. But his voice he kept low, for manners' sake.

> "O, then, I see Queen Mab hath been with you,
> She is the fairies' midwife; and she comes
> In shape no bigger than an agate-stone . . ."

"Bah!" grumbled Ben. "Agate-stones come in all sizes, and this is too much aside from the purpose."

But the teasing, insinuating, damnably enticing voice went on. Ben looked at the faces of the boys, and saw their eyes distended, their mouths open. He looked at old Tom Pope, and saw tears on his cheeks. It should be illegal for any man,

a poet too, with only a grammar school education, to possess a
voice that charmed away people's wits.

> ". . . on the fore-finger of an alderman,
> Drawn with a team of little atomies
> Athwart men's noses as they lie asleep . . ."

"Bah!" said Ben. "What has all this to do with the play?
What's he to her, or she to him?"

"Well, you see, he thinks he's Marlowe," explained Jack
Donne.

"Marlowe!" Ben snorted. "Not like him at all. Faustus in his
chariot, drawn by dragons' heads, was utterly unlike this
country stuff."

"Not a little like Ovid's flea, who creeps into every corner
of a wench? Or sometimes, like a periwig, to sit upon her
brow?"

"Utterly unlike. Marlowe was a scholar," snarled Ben.

"And a brawler, like Mercutio," chimed in Marston, winking
at Donne.

"True, I talk of dreams," Shakespeare was saying,

> "Which are the children of an idle brain,
> Begot of nothing but vain fantasy . . ."

But suddenly he broke off, and stepped over to Ben Jonson.
"I think all that skimble-skamble stuff should be thrown out,"
he whispered. "It is against all classical standards, and I know
not why I should prattle so. All I know of this Mercutio, to tell
the truth, is that he had cold hands."

"No, no, no, no, no," said Ben. "That Queen Mab stuff is
new, bold, original, and smacks of honest country magic —
not book magic, culled out of metaphysics and necromancy,
like Marlowe's."

"Hear him, hear him, hear him," snickered Marston to
Donne. "Mr. Know-all from Wit-well."

"Leave it in, leave it in," Ben said loudly. "One country poet is worth all these afternoon men from the law-courts."

Doubtfully, the country poet went upstage to confer with Heminge and Burbage about this riot between the Capulets and Montagues. For the people with money, who would be coming here to the stylish new Blackfriars Theatre, as well as for the Queen at Greenwich, perhaps the brawls should be softened and prettified. It was not good to have a quarrel (even though licensed for performance by the Master of the Revels) which so much resembled the troublesome affair between the Danvers brothers and the Longs in Hampshire.

"Oh hell, Willy, we've changed it and changed it," Dick Burbage said. "For God's sake, man, are you losing your mettle? What's got thee, these days?"

Shakespeare smiled sadly and shrugged. "In truth I know not why I am so sad," he murmured. "It wearies me, you say it wearies you, but what it derives from, or whereof 'tis made —"

"Put it in a play, put it in a play, let's get on with it, we have all the accounts to settle with Giles Allen before noon," Burbage said, still irritated over having to play Romeo, who was Fortune's fool and would be all London's before the year was out. He liked good murdering parts, villainous, evil parts, wherein the whole ungodly and jungle nature of a man could wallow, and stretch, and exult, and yell ha ha!

So did the audiences, no doubt about it. Was Willy becoming soft with success and his shares in the Burbages' profits?

Well, at least Tibalt would be killed in a few minutes, if they could get on with it. That was good, especially since it would knock this beggarly Jonson out of the play early. Willy could bring no more pussycats and puppydogs home, so lately he had taken to bad actors.

Better call in Cuthbert and have a hard talk with Willy. No money in charity, that was flat.

Marston and Donne were muttering together right below the rail of the stage.

"I think it is old Heironimo's doublet, which we could not

fumigate well enough, and gave to the old-clothes man," Marston was saying.

"Did God make a man to wear breeches so stuffed?" inquired Jack Donne, who was studying for either the priesthood or the ministry, depending which way the money went. You never knew, these days. What if France and Spain resolved their differences again, and poured soldiers into the English counties of the North?

"And Shaky has him so softened he'll melt and fill doublet and breeches too. Look at him simpering there, who once was an honest man," Marston sneered.

Ben heard that. A shiver went through him. He would have knocked their heads together then, if Shakespeare had not summoned him to run over the duel. Three strides for Tibalt, to this crack in the board here. Bounce and spring, parry, tierce, parry, dagger high, when Romeo rushes in.

"Ned, fill in for Nick," said Shakespeare, nodding to Burbage. That well-fed youth, who once had been as pretty as a girl, was getting quite fat, and his face was becoming more ruddy, broad, and coarse. Ben Jonson looked glumly at this famous actor, and felt rage surge up.

"Why all this babble of a wench with a black eye?" he barked. "This Romeo is all patches, not one real humour in his composition. Neither Aristotle, Quintilian, Horace, Ovid, nor any other authority would permit him so to rave about this wench named Rosalind. Besides, Tom Lodge squeezed all the juice out of her with his poem, and our audiences will find her stale."

The players all looked at Shakespeare.

He smiled politely, and drew Burbage aside. "The man is starving," he whispered.

"Damn his eyes, Willy, I'll not stand here and hear more!"

"Let us first feed him, and he'll astound us with well-nourished humours. Moreover, he has a wife and sick baby. Sixth and lastly, the man is a good gadfly, and I need a little stinging."

Burbage lifted his hands and let them fall, slapping his powerful thighs. "God keep me a Christian, or I'll upend the fellow and dump him from yon window."

"After dinner, Dick, let us see how he is transformed. Gentlemen, shall we resume?"

Jonson was pointing out fallacies to any who would even look his way, until the quarrel, the duel, and the unpremeditated murder went off at last. The all-knowing scholar was too rash, he leaped and clanked so hard the new stage shook all over. All grudge and gumption, he whanged through the swordplay like a Hollander in hot armour. Burbage got tired and began breathing too hard. Marston and Donne laughed.

"It seems this cat in stolen clothes has prorumpt the play," Marston said, and the laughter became general.

Jonson was heard explaining that Tibalt was meant to be a man of choleric humour, and he defied any man to tell him otherwise.

"I stand with Aristotle!" he cried.

It was time for someone to do something, and Shakespeare did it. Strolling affably downstage, he took the sweating scholar by the arm and went for a quiet walk with him into the tiring room and down the back stairs for a serious discussion.

When they returned, the red-headed young know-all was curiously changed.

"We'll have the quarrel scene again, boys," Shakespeare said.

But what had become of Jonson's last stand?

Amazing to see how gently he roared his insults now, and with what catlike grace he fenced and parried.

"I wonder what Willy said to him?" whispered Robin Gough.

"I could tell you," whispered Ned.

"What, tell me what?"

"Told him a secret," whispered Ned. But he could not tell Robin what the secret was.

Now the players went quickly through action and lines, and

added the scene of Romeo killing Tibalt. Jonson died so agreeably that Marston could not stand it any longer, but meowed all over the playhouse.

Up shot dead Tibalt, his reformation forgotten, leaped over benches and pounced upon the lawless law-man, shaking him like a rat.

Unfortunately he still had Tibalt's rapier with him, and knew how to use it.

"Help! Save me! Call out the Watch!" whimpered Marston.

Jack Donne, ever a compromiser, as soon as he found out the safe side, was circling the two brawlers, trying to make up his mind which to help. Or, conversely, which to subdue.

A difficult decision! Moreover, the Lord Chamberlain's Men were waiting for Shakespeare to take charge of his cat-man.

"Willy, I leave it to you. He's yours, all yours," Burbage said.

Meanwhile Jonson, his rapier between his teeth, was banging the insolent law-man's noggin against a good knobbly bench.

"Envy and lack of merit in one pestilential person!" he explained, tumbling Marston backward over the bench.

"Willy? Where art thou?" Burbage called.

"It is possible that we did not feed him enough," Shakespeare observed, while sadness sat upon his countenance. He was on his way toward the noisy discussion when it was punctuated by a pistol-shot.

The bullet flew whining by him and nearly got young Ned up in the balcony, who had been enjoying the show and waiting to play Juliet.

Jonson took Marston's pistol from him, hauled him to his feet, chased him downstairs out of the playhouse, back and forth across the great garden, then out into Water Lane past Portinari's parlour, clattering and howling past Lord Cobham's house, past the tennis ground, and then through the very private yards and gardens of that most dreaded old dowager, Lady Russell, setting her shrieking; and at last in, around, out and past the quiet sunny corner in the Lord Chamberlain's yard, where Lord Hunsdon himself had been reclining asleep, and sadly wasted by fever.

No genius, evil or good, might have done worse, or better. Indignant voices began to chatter within private quarters about the outrages perpetrated by these low and vulgar players who had somehow mistakenly been permitted to build, renovate and disturb within the only remaining quality quarter in London.

"Something must be done!"

"Something shall! I give you my word!"

Meanwhile poor Marston, yelling for the Watch, for the constables, for the beadles, for the justices, or even for a little bit of justice itself, had attracted quite a crowd of citizens from the feather-makers' shops, the button-makers' shops, the tennis courts, and the little court of the tinkling conduit, hard by Mr. Smallpiece's house.

"Help! Help! The Watch! It is a riot! Where are the Queen's justices?" screamed the lawless law-man, falling prostrate in the trough of the fountain, splattering out of it, dancing into the cloister alley, until finally he was sent sprawling and bawling with a kick from the red-haired Man of Wrath that would have made any football player a hero.

Acknowledging imaginary applause, Ben Jonson returned through the ranks of staring people, past Lord Chamberlain Hunsdon's house, old Lady Russell's house, past the tennis ground and Lord Cobham's house, up Water Lane, across the great garden, in through the wide doorway of the ancient frater of the Black Friars, up through the crowd of interested idlers and apprentices and into the playhouse.

"Here I am," he said. "I have returned. You may proceed, gentlemen. Where were we?"

chapter seven

🐾🐾 IT was his sad shrew that saved the fierce and scholarly cat-man from the wrath of players, the vengeance of law-men, the justice of gentlemen neighbours.

She came weeping quietly to tell Ben Jonson that their little Mary was dead.

An awful pang went through Shakespeare's heart.

What if it were my own?

The players took up a collection and sent the imperfect husband and grieving father back to the Black Bell Hostelry with his Anne.

"It is in some sort true, I recognize, that I am to a degree inclined to quickness of apprehension, that is to say temper," Ben mumbled as Shakespeare embraced him and wished him well.

So the players went on quietly with their rehearsals, the law-men restrained their man Marston, and the good neighbours of the Blackfriars quarter ceased circulating their petition to the Privy Council.

Things were nearly normal among the players the next week and Ned was doubling for Tibalt as well as giving a perishing performance as Juliet, when Dick Burbage looked up from his death scene in the tomb of the Capulets and uttered a howl.

"Oh God! The classical cat is back!"

The ragged red hair of Ben Jonson was then rising over the edge of the tomb, his pale cadaverous countenance with it.

"Indeed I have returned, my friends. It is my duty," he explained.

Ned fell out of the tomb and Burbage had to go back into the tiring house to see some man about something a long while, and in the confusion it became necessary for Shakespeare to call time for dinner.

60

꽝꽝 IN a silver glitter of light from a thousand candles, in the gorgeous hall of gold, silver, and silken tapestries at Whitehall, the lively ladies of the great Elizabeth's court were swarming about that sweet Mr. Shakespeare and his players after the pitiful play of Juliet and her Romeo.

Penny Rich, the adorable Stella of poor dead Phillip Sidney, Lady Jocosa Carew, Lady Bedford, Lady Bridget Manners, and those two darling young maids of honour from Gawsworth in Cheshire, the sisters Mary and Anne Fitton, were laughing and crying at once, so deliciously sad, so unbearably sweet, so altogether perishing and full of anguish was his play. Through it all the modest man in the Lord Chamberlain's livery of blue and buff smiled and bowed and looked more like a king than any of the gilded courtiers and pompous ambassadors at the festival.

"If he did not play kings in sport he might consort with kings himself," one admiring lady of quality was heard to remark.

"He could consort with me any time," Lady Jocosa answered, her bold black eyes flashing. It was true that she was given to extravagant statements, all of which were immediately discounted by those that knew her, including, alas, her husband. Including also the modest man from Stratford. Born only a mile from her noble castle of Clopton House, he had never allowed himself to forget the distance between the son of a yeoman and the wife of a lord.

Or had he?

"I know for a fact, he had her in the bushes one night at the Gray's Inn Revels."

"Only one night?"

"The lady swooned with joy as he taught her poetry."

"Only poetry?"

A buzz and a twitter followed his dignity and mocked it, but that was the way of flatterers and fawners at court.

"Wrote twenty sonnets to some black wench. She's not black in the face, whatever she is in deeds."

"Black as hell and dark as night, he said. That he did."

"Must have been one of those blackamoors' wenches that Tom Baskerville brought in from Porto Rico."

"I'd believe it. These players will do anything."

"Ought to take all these blackamores right out of the realm before any more can lie with 'em. God will never bless this land if we do not keep it for the kind of people He put here."

"Right, right. Drive 'em out I say, all Jews and Portygees too."

"Right again. It's our country. No foreigners here."

"Look at that Shakespeare man now, ogling the new maids of honour. I heard he lay with Lucy Morgan, the Queen's favourite until she was banished for lechery. Will no one keep these players down?"

Mistress Mary Fitton, the newest and merriest maid of honour, whispered sweet nothings into the great Mr. Shakespeare's left ear while Lady Jocosa goaded him in his right.

Or were they nothings? They might be somethings.

The gay and giddy crowd of permitted people swarmed about the dazzling throne in the Paradise Chamber, studded with diamonds, rubies and sapphires, beneath the gilded ceilings and in the swooning glory of the great Queen's very presence, drinking in every rustle and whisper, all eyes for everything of greatness and beauty and glory. A heavy weight of adoration hung upon this one small woman in her stiff embroidered gown, her heavy necklace of pearls, her glittering tiara and headrail like a flight of half-invisible wings about her poor human head. Painted all white and rose, her thin face could not smile without cracking the layers of white lead, vinegar, milk of green figs, alum, and gum arabic, with the proper red fucus laid on thickly with white poppy oil.

Great God, who had painted the old woman this time? Kneeling before the legendary lady, the respectful Mr. Shake-

speare suspected that merry Mistress Mary who kept tickling
and pinching his arm to make him trip in his speech of gratitude. Her reckless ways might get her into trouble with this
stern old woman in the frizzed red wig, whose haunted dark
eyes now stared down at her servant Shakespeare kneeling
before her.

If she but dared look in a mirror, she'd crack, he thought.
A quarter-century ago he had dared to look into these same
haunted eyes when the Queen had visited his beloved master,
the Fat Knight of Warwick. A boy of eight then, a woman
near forty winters. Now I'm thirty-one, and she's for the ages.
Weary and gaunt-looking then, on that green hillside below
Earl Ambrose's castle, her heavy burden of care already too
great for one frail woman. God pity her now, as I pitied her
then. And God forgive her for her Privy Council's cruelty in
the name of gentle Jesus.

And once more he saw the bloody quarters of the martyred
Southwell on the crimson scaffold, and heard the roars of the
crowd.

Alas, that ever the Pope called on Englishmen to deny their
Queen and country!

It cannot come to any good, no matter how many priests
are tortured in Topcliffe's house.

I hear he has access to her in her private apartments at all
hours, and they laugh together over his tortures.

Can this be?

Oh, my poor cousin Arden, and poor Lopez done to death
for gossip, and Robin Debdale for sorcery! Who next?

It might be my mother or father, or any woman who craves
confession for her sins and peace for her soul.

God forgive us all. This poor woman would only be moder-
ate and gracious if these savage Christians would forbear to
rend one another.

"Stop muttering in thy beard and attend her," whispered
his secret mistress, Lady Jocosa. Or was it a secret?

Who would dream it? he thought, and became aware of the
Queen's incredibly fresh young voice speaking straight to him,

that voice that had made his heart leap with love and joy when first he heard it, and sounded no less wonderful now.

"We meet again, Mr. Shakespeare," she was saying, while the painted lips smiled and he saw her black teeth. "And neither I nor any one of my astrologers came near ten miles of your invention, though some learned fellows predicted it would be another night of errors like your last. But I have heard some good speeches about you, and in truth I know two professions you are master in. You can write sweeter music than any I have ever heard, save in Latin, and you are a better surgeon than any man in my retinue. I have forgot my swooning head and my jumping teeth, and I do think I shall sleep tonight. You are a right trusty and most mellifluous master of all sorrows and joys that may be communicated to an old woman's heart in words. Pray mind thy health, sweet Mr. Shakespeare, for I would see more of thy plays before I die. Mr. Burbage!"

"Here, Gracious Unparalleled Majesty!" said Dick, who had been stealing voluptuous glances into the silk purse which old Pertybeard Knollys, Controller of the Royal Household, had bestowed upon the players.

"Good Romeo, see that thy Shakespeare is well nourished."

"Celebrated Majesty, it shall be done! We'll cram him to the eyes with chops and hog-jowls, and stuff him till he cracks."

Elizabeth answered him in Greek, and he forgot what he was going to say for the first time in his life. Then she rose from her jewelled throne, giving her hand to the handsomest of all her handsome young men, Robert Devereux, the Earl of Essex. And all her brilliant train, in their gorgeous and glowing tints, followed slowly with mincing steps over the sweet-smelling herbs of lavender, rosemary and bay strewn upon the floors in preparation for a night of dancing.

The lutes, the viols, the bandores, citterns and drums struck up the light lavolta, and not one of the merry ladies leaped as high as the Queen.

Rain, hail, snow, and a howling wind from the north came down soon after, breaking the spell of lovely swooning weather that had brought the spirit of spring to the month of Janus, that two-faced god of beginnings. Whirling sparks and columns of smoke blew in from the great fireplaces in the shining halls, and candle flames flickered in coronas, chandeliers and wall sconces. On went the dancing, gayer and faster as the night pressed down on the giddy ladies and their lords, and even the players joined in country rounds and flauntings. All hope of floating down the river at ebb tide to Paul's Wharf from here in Westminster on the players' barge, or even of being towed by a brace of dray-boats, had been given over, and fine ladies were dancing with players by now while their lords replenished their flagging energies with ypocras, huffcap, capri, clary, muscadel and malvesy.

But here here, this mingling with low and vulgar players would never do!

My Lord of Southampton, my Lord of Essex, my Lord of Rutland confabulated alcoholically together.

"By my George and Garter, Willy, it was you who raised this Shakescene up so high, when you first stooped and took him." This from Essex, the uncommonly vain and handsome plaything of the Queen, so that he was nervous between times, and itching for any occasion of a quarrel.

Moreover, his sister Penny simply would not stay in the bed he had made for her with the rich Lord Rich, but was always cavorting off to beget another bastard with Mountjoy.

Somebody should pay for it! Swollen with drinking, his hot eyes followed the vulgar players, so gaily jumping with high ladies.

"If her Majesty had not begun it, our wenches would not want to consort with such scum," said Roger Manners, Lord Rutland, whose voice still went rather shrill when he was goosed or goaded.

Young Southampton, with his long curls so carefully crimped by his barber and falling over his left shoulder, declared that after all, he had not given Shakespeare anything yet, and might not. But it amused him to toy with the fellow's expectations.

"That is one word for it I've never heard," said the handsome Ralegh, who had been leaping with the Queen, and had now come to brag over his rivals.

"Shall we take the Fitton sisters?" asked Essex, moving away from the Devon braggart in his black and silver.

"Fitten enough," Southampton said, and they went off arm in arm among the dancers to take the prettiest ladies away from the vulgar players.

Meanwhile an unwieldy and uncouth monster with red hair, who had been scolding the fairy-boys and snubbing the ladies all evening, now plodded glumly among the players' properties, stuffing them in great wicker baskets for the return journey down the Thames, whenever it was to be.

"A man like me, stuck with such menial duties," he snarled, throwing in banqueting stuff from Capulet's feast, mixed in with candle-sconces for the funeral or wedding, whatever it was between Romeo and his Juliet. "Bah, bah, bah," said Ben Jonson.

A wandering highborn lady, dizzy with drink and dancing, overheard him mumbling among the properties and stopped to fling a little extra wit at him.

"Tibalt, my dear! I thought you were dead."

Ben Jonson scowled at Penelope Rich, the dissolute sister of the haughty Essex. Her famous golden hair, celebrated by Philip Sidney, seemed to have been touched up with gilt. Her black eyes looked swollen and bleary.

"I might as well be," Ben said.

A lovely piece though, from what he could tell. A pity she and Sidney never did it. Now, if I wrote puling love-sonnets, by God we'd do it in every one. I'd make that a rule.

"I enjoyed your dying. Do you enjoy your living?"

"No," said Ben, tossing in some of the apothecary's flasks.

"Why not? Have you no wench in the kitchens or somewhere? It's a cold night."

"And may you all freeze in it," said Ben, glaring at her with such classical scorn that the lady quite twitched.

"Heavens! The man hates me. You hate the play, I could see it. I think it was not Romeo's sword but your own fat spleen that killed you."

Ben ignored all insults from wenches, however high the wenches or low the taunts.

"The play is all wrong and any fool knows it. It is against the best classical standards," he informed her.

Penny sat down on a basket, almost toppling it and going petticoats-over-head inside.

She recovered some dignity anyhow. "What standards, pray, are the best classical standards?"

"Aristotle's," Ben snarled, hissing the admired name. "Horace. Even our Sidney."

He eyed her close. H'm, if she'd gone in the basket and stayed there, what a bed for the night!

Penelope tittered. "He may have been your Sidney, but he was never mine. He wrote me a number of perishing sonnets, wailing my black eyes and hard heart, but the poor foolish boy . . ."

She leaned up to him, so that he could see her tender breasts in there, quite as good as a kitchenmaid's.

Penny whispered, "He never, never asked me. If he only had, I'd have tumbled in the nearest haycock with him. I do believe the darling boy would have enjoyed it."

Ben snorted. "Humph. Women do not belong in poetry, above the age of sixteen. They're irremediably ruined from that age on."

Penny laughed, then hiccuped.

"How do you know, little tib-cat?"

"I ought to," Ben said. "I've ruined enough."

She cared nothing about his ruining of kitchenmaids. But it amused her to pick and pry into the hidden souls of players and playwrights. She did believe they had them.

"Really now," she murmured. "This Shakespeare man, is he not utterly charming? So gentle . . ."

Ben sniffed.

"So kind . . ."

Ben snorted.

"Everything a woman could want, and goes like a prince about his business. And he can write better about love than any man in history. Ah, women need lovers like that."

"Bah! Copybook love. I lay you a wager he would not know what to do if you crawled into his bed."

"Nor would I," Penny said, jumping up and almost tumbling down into the basket. "His golden wit quite shatters my con-con-concupisness."

"I'll tell him," Ben said, tossing in some cork-soled pumps.

"You are not an old cat nor a fat cat, yet you sound like an old fat cat, and you are little better than a dead cat," Penny said, and went sailing away like a ship with all sails a-flap.

Ben grinned to himself and tossed in some hats, shoes, masks and false noses.

"That will tickle her catastrophe," he said.

But he was lonely, and sighed often, thinking of the ignorance and blindness of a world that could not see the excellence that went unknown, unhonoured and impoverished among the rich and foolish.

By midnight most of the players had crawled into their straw in the tiltyard stables, where old Knollys had granted them permission to pass the night. The storm was now cracking the limbs of quince trees and sycamores, and strewing the trained boughs of old lime trees across King's Street and over the sodden tennis courts.

But where was their Shakespeare?

The Mistress of the Wardrobes had given him a couch behind some hangings near the linen closet, and not far from the sleeping quarters of her Majesty's maids of honour.

He listened to the wind moaning and whispering in the tapestries, and sank into sleep. He lay drowned in sleep, and was just beginning to dream, when somebody leaned down close and kissed him on the lips.

"I've come to thank you, sweet Mercutio," she whispered, as the wind moaned and flapped in the tapestries and sudden gusts shook the frail walls of the flimsy palace old Harry the Thief had erected next to the priory he had stolen from the Dominicans.

"Three and six makes eight and nine," he murmured, still drowned. He was dreaming of money, great heaps of it, growing higher all the time.

"Dear man, dreaming of my kisses," she sighed, crawling in with him.

He was sinking in the sea, to the depths of mindless peace.

"Oh sweet Mercutio, is not this better than groaning for love? Speak to me of love, my dreamer . . ."

"Swift as a shadow, short as any dream . . ."

"Ah, you devil, it is long, like my sad hours without you . . ."

Her sighs and moans became more fervid as they sank into the mindless depths together.

Did they sleep, at last?

He never knew when she left him, with three last kisses, to seal their secret forever.

Sometime in the pale between-time, neither night nor morning, he awoke to see another female form bending over him.

"Thank you for the lovely play, darling Mercutio," she whispered. And she was in, or halfway in. Her teeth were chattering, and she was very cold.

"You are too generous," he mumbled to the hopeful lady. Unfortunately his words became lost in an alarming clatter as she tripped herself up in the sheets and fell out of bed.

Struggling out to assist her, he became entangled too, with the result that they went down together, rolling into the tapestry and beyond it, right up against the creaking wall.

"You goose! You've roused the Queen!"

"And that is not all, either."

"I fear we'll be hanged for this."

"Then let us make the most of it," he said. Amidst smothered laughter, and in total darkness, they did.

"Remember me, but not too much," she giggled, as she fought her way out from behind the tapestry, and was gone.

Oh Lord, they'll kill me with kindness, he thought as he limped back to bed.

Her Majesty was right. I must mind my health.

chapter nine

ꕔꕔ "MAKE way for Milady's coach! Make way there!"

The well-rewarded begetter of Romeo and Juliet managed to jump into the ditch just in time.

There she went, the painted, pampered darling, three long-eared lap dogs in her arms, her running footmen making way for the coach of the rich Lord Rich's wife.

Was that just the flick of an eye-beam toward the muddy player as the pretty Penny swept by? The coach's iron-shod wheels showered him with mud and water, and he heard the high yapping of her fretful spaniels, Tray, Blanche and Sweetheart, mingled with the clopping of hoofs and the cracking of whips.

"Avaunt, you curs! A plague of all candied tongues that lick the rich and great!"

On went the coach toward Essex House in the Strand, where Milady would no doubt soon be seeing and confiding in her confessor.

God grant that the other one will not be confiding in her husband. They flattered me like a dog. When the rain comes to wet me, and the wind to make me chatter, and when the thunder will not peace at my bidding, there I shall find 'em, there I'll smell 'em out. They told me I was everything, but that's a lie. I am not ague-proof.

A mincing dame, with a face of virtue gone as sour as if it had been steeped in lingering pickle, also threw him a glance as she went past him, switching her tail.

From the waist down they are centaurs, though women all above.

Fie on 'em all! No more, though I live to be a lean and slippered pantaloon cackling in my chimney corner. And if I do not find that golden gate at some riotous wench's favour soon, or my giddy patron's hand, old age will take me to my grave before I ever get Anne her manor house.

To work! To work!

The players were not at Blackfriars at all today. The carpenters and plasterers wanted better wages. He hailed a wherry at Paul's Wharf and crossed the river to smell wet plaster and watch the new Swan take wing against the sordid shapes of the leaping-houses on Love Lane.

Could we do it? Should we do it? Shall we do it?

I'll beard Dick Burbage and the cautious Cuthbert and put it to them straight.

And then he went plodding on through mud and snow to see Mistress Martha, as she was called, still lying sick in the Marshalsea among the whores and rogues, not to speak of the captured missionary priests and scurvy players.

"My old friend John Sore would go bond. He told me so," Shakespeare whispered. "If you could endure a public house until our friends can pay off the Queen's Inquisitor."

"Anywhere, my dear," murmured the frail lady. Her small delicate hand, like a bird's claw, touched his for a moment and she closed her eyes to sleep, if she could.

He threw a bawdy jest to the turnkey on his way out of the accursed place, and was rewarded with a leer and a laugh.

What a pair, he thought. Doll Sore, who'll go any man for a shilling or come to quits without it when she's hot, and this tortured saint almost transparent with fasting and care.

Well, my giddy wanton's mother wants to be loved for nothing, but she is generous for all that. I'll let old John Sore pay the bond and who'll ever suspect where it came from?

I'll off to Tichfield as soon as we've wound up our business in Curtain Close.

As he hurried home to Holywell Street in the glimmering dark of early evening, the dirty snow looked green against the flaring lamps and torches of the taverns and alehouses.

Strange, he thought. That old man is following me.

My conscience is usually an old lady.

Each time he warily turned around, the tail of a skulking form flicked behind a cart, beyond a penthouse, or it melted among a crowd of carts, horses and plodding people.

Three times he would have sworn that a tall old man with red-rimmed evil eyes, a beard like a rubbing-brush, wearing a puce velvet cloak and a steeple-crowned hat, was eagerly peering out at him from the faceless swarm.

Old Topcliffe himself is on my trail. I'll fox him if I have to move in with Doll myself. Or leave my Lord and his mother and become plain Shagspear of Stratford, without their hundred pounds.

No, no, never, never, never. My son must be a gentleman yet. Then let the proud wenches spatter us with mud if they will.

Perhaps I could do it for eighty pounds.

Get three loads of stone from the quarries out Hampton Heath way, and mend the walls and walks. I must have a garden and an orchard.

After all, my daughters must be ladies, and not soil their dainty shoes.

A small red-nosed boy clopped past him on wooden clogs to keep his tender toes from the muddy snow.

Like my own Hamnet, but not as handsome. What a Prince Hamlet *he* could play, in a few long creeping years! Ten years old now, and in his fourth year of Latin. Gentler with the teachers than I ever was. More of his mother's gentleness. Ah God, will he ever forgive me for being no father all this weary while?

The humblest cobbler in Stratford does better for his bairns than I. Why not give it up and go home? We could move back into the central house over the orchard. Though after the awful fire last year there's fifty good houses ruined, and my father needs tenant money.

Why went I not to school to study money, money, money? Fie on all poetry. It makes you a companion to drabs and ditches.

Well, I'll teach my Hamnet better sense. His name reminds me over and over of that Danish prince who killed his uncle for poisoning his father and lying with his mother, and set fire to the castle before he had done with his fitful fever.

Strange haunting I have from that bloody story. Why will it mutter in my ears of its mouldy passions centuries ago?

Rest, rest, perturbed spirit!

Amleth they called him, in the oldest accounts, but Tom Kyd named him Hamlet.

All bright things come to confusion, and are one with darkness.

What is it in Penny's distracted and wasteful life that steeps me in pity, though she would laugh if I dared say so? They say her uncle Leicester poisoned her father before he bedded her mother. And poor Amy Robsart too, they used to whisper in Warwickshire.

That proud and haughty brother of hers will boy the Queen too far one day, and the old lady will tumble him in the mud.

Or the executioner his head.

Poor fancy's followers are we all. Thrice-blessed they that master their wild blood. A plague on me for a poperin poet, I'm quoting myself. Better set to work on a new fiddle-faddle ere I wear old strings quite through.

But which? What new news at Court? What latest gossip in Paul's? They say young Essex will be the Queen's general if the French goad the old woman into a seige this spring.

I might cobble up Peele's old play of the troublesome reign of King John. We fought the Frogs well then, and no doubt we will again, and again, and again.

But when he broached the subject of moving to the Bank-side, the Burbages and Tom Pope were against it.

"What, leave our investments to rot in Shoreditch?"

"I smell a cold wind coming, boys. And Langley will not use the Swan this year."

"Money speaks, Willy. And where's the money?"

Shakespeare lifted his shoulders high, put on his cloak, and took a different route to his workshop in Tassel's Close, over a clothmaker's shop. The tall old man was waiting for him in the gloomy doorway.

Shakespeare felt the chilly wind again. Evil glared at him out of this cruel and greedy countenance, revealed to him under a darkening sky, on a street as treacherous as the steep road to hell.

Topcliffe, the Queen's torturer, the most feared and hated man of righteousness in the kingdom.

"A happy evening, Mr. Topcliffe," Shakespeare said, lifting his cap.

"It might be happier for you, Mr. Shakespeare," said the old inquisitor, squinting his rheumy and red-rimmed eyes, and grinning like a dog.

It is most true that Evil wears his own ugly countenance, Shakespeare thought. This devil looks what he is, and yet he'll smile, and smile, and think himself a charmer.

"Then let us be merry, and good night," Shakespeare said, and made as if to enter the doorway of his no longer secret sanctuary.

"You spent a merry night at Whitehall, I think," Mr. Topcliffe said.

"More merry than this with you," Shakespeare said, smiling back. "Or than some friends of mine have spent in your charge."

Blue fire shone in the crafty old torturer's squinting eyes. "Ah, you admit knowing traitors and poisoners."

"God knows such poor sinners better than I. If you have business with me, I pray you speak to the point, and briefly."

Topcliffe rubbed his bony hands, which could never be washed clean of blood if he scoured them a thousand years.

"You have powerful friends still, Mr. Shakespeare. Beware lest they fall from grace."

"I fear nothing from your hands nor any words from your mouth, Mr. Topcliffe. Good night."

"You could prosper greatly, Mr. Shakespeare. All your late troubles could be lifted from your neck," muttered the old man eagerly, leaning so close that Shakespeare drew back from the foul breath of evil, as from a vulture's cruel beak.

"I am not your man, Mr. Topcliffe, and never shall be. If you have words for any friends of mine, let them hear them straight."

"Not many would dare bait me as you do, Mr. Shakespeare. What is it makes you think yourself immune?"

"No more than you, Mr. Topcliffe. Under the eye of God we crawl equal."

"When you see Lady Rich, commend me to her — and Lady Carew, Mr. Shakespeare. Or their confessors." With this sudden word, sneered out with hateful venom, the old man grinned again, beckoned to a pair of low and beastly grooms, who would slit you up and gut you without a blink, drew his velvet cloak about him, and led his men out of Tassel's Close and down Hog Lane.

Still shaking with awful fear, the fortunate playwright, the darling of many an amorous lady, and now pushed right up to the edge of the pit and looking into its fiery mouth, leaned against an alehouse lattice and heard the fearful pounding of his heart.

All, all, thrown away in one gaudy night!

But who put him on me?

And how does he know that poor Jocosa, and the giddy Penelope, have been seeing Father Gerard in the darkest secrecy?

My God, my God, I have been a poor sneaking fool.

I have heard that there is a fear beyond any I have yet known or studied, even. My cousin Southwell must have dared it, at the end. They said he smiled and blessed the executioner, and women wept and wailed to see his heart torn out.

Oh God, when shall thy Son hearken to his people?

When will I sleep in peace again, who have put them on my track? And poor merry ladies, who still would live like holy nuns, if they but dared.

But who put him upon me?

Still trembling, hearing his teeth chatter like a captive monkey's in a cage, he went up the stairs to his once precious hiding place, where he had often worked straight through the night to untie the knots in a tangled plot, or tease fair words out of some foul old story. Then with the morning he would stroll to the playhouse, innocent as a new egg, and when the players asked him to improvise a new scene, he would spin off his nightwork for them, and laugh in his secret soul at how they were fooled.

Old Heminge's eyes pop like an old town bull's when a new heifer is led to him, and he says, "By God, our Willy hath no better in all nature! What his mind thinks, he utters with easiness. Hear him, ye lucky people!"

Oh, I have been a poor trusting fool. Some creeping spy, some informer . . .

But who?

And where will poor Ned and I go now? They pursue us in every quarter, and will not let us live.

He shrugged his shoulders and went into his now useless sanctuary, entering the room as he would a stage. Give no sign of fear. Whistle, hum a tune, smile, look as happy as a smug bridegroom.

And let the spies eat the air, for we'll be gone ere they come again.

"They've been here," his brother whispered, looking at him with eyes full of terror.

"And so have we," Shakespeare said. His lips were too stiff

to whistle, but he managed to hum the tune of *Greensleeves*.

"Oh, Willy, if they followed me it's my fault. I'll cut my throat. Give me thy sword."

"We're not Romans, Neddie. Mere English. And sons of John Shakespeare of Stratford. Would *he* cringe? Would *he* tremble?"

"No, but what is your hand doing, Willy?"

"Remember the Ardens! Oh, my boys, my boys, never forget . . ." And his voice aped the musical accents of their mother so perfectly that Ned gave a weak titter, almost a laugh. "You are not as other people, my dears, for your pedigree is half-good, and through my family, the great and famous Ardens, you come straight from the great Guy of Warwick, the great Athelstan, King of the Saxons, and ah, my darlings, from Alfred the Great himself. Oh, why did I forget it and marry a Shagsbeer?"

"Well, that's not the question, Willy," Ned said, feeling better. "They went through your papers and took some of your books."

"Pitch and sulphur! What hellish fiends have unleashed their foul and undigested evil upon my innocent neck?"

"Quiet, quiet, calm, calm, for God's sake, Willy, or they'll be back," Ned muttered, trying to hold his suddenly wild and furious brother.

"Now all the dogs of war arise and whoop halloo! Trumpets! Trumpets! Arise, ye fire-eyed maid of smoky war! And thou, great heroes of dusty books, aid me, assist, assist," muttered the dazed descendant of King Alfred, King Athelstan, and old Dick Shakyspear of Snitterfield, tossing boots, shirts, stockings, and what books had been spared him into a sack.

"Willy, could we — ?"

"Speak, old boy, name it and we'll do it. The future is ours."

"Willy, what about your rich friends? Why cannot we go there?"

"They might become poor in a night. What if we led the dogs to them?"

"Then where, Willy?"

Ned was helping him pack their few belongings.

"I know a house where not even a cat could sneak in upon us."

"Where?"

But Shakespeare put his finger to his lips, and they did not speak again until they stole away in darkness and into the cold rain.

Deposition befor Courte of
Worshippful Magistrate
Salomon Saltonstall
Byshopsgayte

The Petty collectors within the Warde of Byshopsgate, upon their corporall oathes upon the holye Evangelists of All mighty God, dyd saye & affirme that William Shackspere, of St Ellens parishe, ys ether dead, departed, and gone out of the sayde warde or his goodes soe eloigned or conveyd out, or in suche a pryvate or coverte manner kept, thatte he is in default of due & lawfull payement upon his goodes valued at five pounds the summe of five shillings and all justices of the boros and wardes are praied to apprehend & seek out the same in the name of God his Saintes & Apostles, Amen From the Court this xvth of February in this yeere of our Ladie Elizabeths peace the xlviii.

Book Two
🐏🐏

UNCERTAIN

GLORY

O, how this spring of love resembleth
  The uncertain glory of an April day,
Which now shows all the beauty of tho sun,
  And by and by a cloud takes all away!

The Two Gentlemen of Verona,
I, III

chapter ten

❦❦ THE long dark gloom-time of Lent shut down on the players for forty days.

Old man Henslowe sent two constables to arrest Ben Jonson for debt.

"Justice! Help! Justice!" howled Ben, digging his heels in the mud of Holywell Lane.

"For God's sake, what is it now?" asked Dick Burbage, running out.

"Send for Shakespeare! Inform Shakespeare that his closest adviser is being taken away!" Ben yelled.

"He's gone to the country, and so would I too, if I had the money," Burbage said.

"You cannot spare me! I am needed here! In simple justice, explain that I cannot be parted from my many duties!" Ben advised him at the top of his voice while grinning boobies and dolls of the quarter came flocking to see the show.

"We've had nothing but brawls and bragging since you first

cursed us with your classical presence," Burbage informed the plunging poet. "You may be spared. Take him with you, boys, a long way off."

"Justice! Justice! Where in this pestilent kingdom is any justice?" Ben was still crying as the constables dragged him away.

By the time they had conveyed him across the Thames in a scavenger boat, and all the way down Bear Alley and Maid Lane to old man Henslowe's counting house, the two constables were all tired out, and were sick of the classics too.

"Well, Benjamin, I hope you've brought me my two acts I paid you for," said the famous churchwarden and money-lender, as Ben came snarling and stumbling in.

"Oh Lord, sir, here's the worst one we ever did take, and his language is that horrible too," groaned the first constable, ready to lie down.

"Thirty years serving her Majesty and the justices of this borough and I've never seen such a lewd knave. I've said it afore, and I'll say it again, what is this country coming to, with such younkers in it?" inquired the second constable.

"Is that all you want, Mr. Henslowe?" asked the delinquent monster, leering, which would have been pleasant except that he looked worse that way than plain glum.

"That's all I want, Benjamin, my boy," said Henslowe, rubbing his hands and looking benevolent: for after all he was a churchwarden.

"Why, if I had not been so pressed, and so sweated, and so frantic, helping my friend Shakespeare bring forth his last play, I would have had your two little acts for you, sir, last week. How could these brains have forgotten?"

"Show me how the same brains can quickly beget my two acts, or into the Marshalsea you go, my boy, and this time even Mistress Martha cannot save you."

Ben's jaw dropped and hung there. For one time in his life he had no words ready, even from the classics.

But how did the churchwarden know?

Great saints and martyrs, my neck is in his knobby hands!

But one nod from him to the torturers, and I am racked, drawn on a hurdle, whipped, bound, delivered to the hangman, strung up, cut down, degutted, quartered and hung up at the four corners of the kingdom.

Oh God, poor Mrs. Lynn! I was to go to her and be of some comfort, and I am that low, brutish and stupefied that I did not do that which all conscience required me to do.

"Well, Benjamin? Well? Well?" Henslowe was squawking.

Ben gulped down all the anger he had left, wagged his big ragged head up and down, signifying submission, and humbly took his place at the second assistant copy clerk's desk in the back office, to finish what he should have finished, and do what he should have done — the last two acts of *The Isle of Dogs*, for which he had already been paid.

Ben disregarded, too, the rude remarks of Henry Chettle, Thomas Dekker, and young Will Houghton, other obedient slaves of the whoremaster, that is to say, playwrights.

"We've never had a play-cobbler in stuffed breeches."

"Perhaps there are two of him?"

"Then one could be spared to assist sweet Mr. Shakespeare?"

"Perhaps one end of this one?"

"Which would be more suitable for Mr. Shakespeare?"

"Ah, a nice question."

"We could ascertain which end talks."

"How should we address it?"

"It might bite."

Tears slowly dripped from the end of Ben's nose onto the paper. What a foul script Tom Nashe had left him to finish! Rain, rain, on the roof of old man Henslowe's counting house, cold rain on the river, in the marshes and the pools and ditches of the Bankside, cruel rain on the new grave of little Mary, an impudent and lewdly intended play, as might be expected from Tom the parson's son, who had already scandalized the town with his biting pamphlets and lascivious verses.

This thing could be called seditious, with its gibes at Court and Council.

If I were a free man, I would not touch it.

After I have finished this, I will cobble no more for Mr. Henslowe and his company.

Oh, my poor shrew! My little Mary, child of our youth!

And all this time that Stratford cobbler is idling and bridling it in the luxury and lechery of Hampshire, with his doting lord and the pretty lord's prettier mother! *He* has a son! And does he care one hoot for him? A naughty earl, that is *his* lovely boy!

Oh, I shall split with spleen!

But on his solitary and muttering walk through the rain, nodding and shaking his big matted head, shrugging his scarecrow shoulders, winking and grimacing at his thoughts and agreeing with all of them, the bitter Ben went blindly stumbling among the ignorant hordes of common English stinkards, on his way to find the holy woman at the Marshalsea, if she lived.

"It is nevertheless my mission to reform wrong thinking in these corrupted times," he explained to himself. "Who are they? Empty scribblers! Bacon-brains! Piddlers in Pie Corner! Apes of a besotted age! May the gut-gripe grind 'em all!"

A warm bare arm slid inside his ragged cloak, with an amorous tickling hand.

"That's what I tell 'em, dear, that's what I call them," cooed a female voice. Loose lips smiled up into his face, dark eyes sparkled like topazes. "Come along, love, we'll damn the whole pack of 'em together, will we, chuck?"

The exact sum of money in his pocket totted itself up in his angry head.

"I'd be your man if I had the money, wench," he muttered quickly. "I pray, excuse me until next week?"

"Hang thee, stinkard! What, with that face?" she sneered, and her laughter followed him a little way down Love Lane, tempering his literary indignation with a more piercing pain. I'll just stop at Doll Sore's house and have a pint, he decided, easier on himself now under this humiliation.

And he hurried into the Boar's Head before his conscience should catch up with him.

Here in this warm and friendly place, sliding his famished trunk and shanks along a polished bench at the rear of the taproom, among watermen and scavengers of the quarter, he eagerly whipped out his notebook and scribbled in it.

"Ah, they'll see some day, they'll learn," he mumbled. "And all their seasons, tempers and distempers will I brew, until I have all their evil nature in a pot."

He was scratching away there, amazing himself with his mental splendour, when a new boy in the house nudged him rather smartly in the brisket.

"What will you drink, sir?"

Ben lifted his rocky head and snarled, "Keep thy paws to thyself, thou stinkard!"

"Mistress Dolly says you owe her too much money to scratch any more words in her house."

"What, you egg! Who sent thee?"

"I'm seeking my father, sir, and I thought you might know him."

The last words spoken softly, with piercing earnestness, as the boy studied the scribbled words in the notebook.

"Who art thou?" Ben said, with sudden gentleness.

"I'm Mr. Shakespeare's boy, sir."

The surly scholar dropped the notebook.

"Boy, tell me no lies. I know him, and he has no boy."

"He'll have me though," the boy said. "As soon as he comes home."

A wary silence fell between them, as the lean and hungry scholar eyed the boy.

"What's thy name?"

"Hamnet, sir, but my father calls me Hamlet."

Great God the Father, Ben thought, still eyeing this small, pale, frail boy. The same bearing, the same trick of the nether lip, the identical droop of the eyelids — and, beaming with too much intelligence, the eyes were ready to be mocking or merry, or melt the heart with sorrow.

"Did he send you to mock me?"

Young Hamnet started back at the menace in his voice. Mistress Dolly had been noticing them and was elbowing her way forward.

"You've run away to find him? Tell the truth."

"There's no time to tell lies," Hamnet said, and then the angry hostess had reached the table and sent him to the kitchen, all in one short speech which also included Ben Jonson and his origins, his low and degenerate associations, and a dark and squalid future to begin immediately and end promptly if he did not pay the screaming woman those two pounds seven and six he owed her, and owed her, and owed her until it was more than a Christom body could stand.

So that night he did not have a pint after all at Doll Sore's house, but as he continued his interrupted journey to the prison, the hungry scholar was beginning to see a little light on the road back to Shoreditch and the Lord Chamberlain's Men.

But now, what about a quick stop at the Elephant Inn, where the Italian travellers congregated? A little warmth first, a little laughter.

ꙍꙍ DUST and ashes were blowing about in the Great Hall of Tichfield House, the Earl of Southampton's castle on the misty downs of Hampshire. A cold wind howled on the heath and whipped the waters of the cattail-marshes. Wind rippled in the Arras tapestries and sent gusts of smoke out of the fireplaces into people's faces.

What a night for *A Midsummer Night's Dream!*

"Oh, I'll perish of this villainous spring!" sobbed Lady Southampton, the unfortunate mother of the errant Earl. Why had she ever commissioned this mocking play for a country performance at Tichfield? Particularly in this weather?

These rude squires, who could talk only of rotting corn and ruined profits, these feather-headed lords eager for war and booty, always off to the taverns or sodden with drink at home — who were they to sit quietly through a play of fairies and monsters in love? The thing was a mockery anyhow: first performed at her wedding in a hailstorm two years ago, and that husband lasted only a year! Alas, poor old Mr. Hencage! Even his name had not taken sufficiently to last!

What could a twice-widowed lady do?

And who could control her carousing son? Still on a boar hunt, or tippling in taverns with his lover-boys, his hairy sailors, his scum of the seas?

"His Lordship promised me on his honour he would be home for the pageant!" wailed the widowed lady, wringing her hands.

A cringing secretary; a fawning tutor; the boys of Blackfriars sneezing and coughing in the artificial forest of green boughs and sweet-smelling herbs prepared for the pageant; the uneasy invited company huddled upon their benches and muttering about going home.

Florio the tutor, really a spy planted on her by the Queen,

shrugged his fat shoulders. Roper the secretary looked at Mr. Shakespeare, who was to blame for all this; as for Mr. Shakespeare, he was composing a sonnet about watching the clock for his absent patron.

> *Being your slave, what can I do but wait*
> *And watch the bloody clock for you . . . sweet boy . . .*
> *I have no precious time at all to spend*
> *Until I have the wherewithal to buy*
> *That big old house in Stratford for my wife . . .*

Needs polish. I'll never get the money that way.

But he became aware that people were waiting for him to give the word for the pageant to begin.

"Dear Mr. Shakespeare! Save me!"

The widowed lady seized his hand and gazed imploringly into his eyes.

He nodded to the musicians in the gallery. They began the consort of music for the opening dance. Out from their bower came the vestals in their modest costumes.

The flutey voices of the highborn ladies made a rather thin thing of their chorus.

That sweet Mr. Shakespeare felt his neck getting hot, and muttered curses that would blister their pretty ears, if the highborn ladies had only heard.

Wise already in the ways of low-talented ladies, he never presumed to lead them in their songs and dances, but always to praise them in high astounding terms. But his boys would catch it when he put them through their paces, later, when it came time for the low and vulgar players to perform.

Then, too, his alert eye penetrated the mask of the liveliest lady of the troop (indeed they did in some sort resemble their horses) and knew she was the intended bride.

Alas, poor Liz!

The amorous and energetic daughter of old Sir John Vernon of Hodnet, who had been lurking in Southampton's walks for two years, until he had inadvertently tumbled over her in the bushes. It was believed the lady tripped him.

The doomed young lord had been running away from her ever since, with less and less conviction.

What was it? A fascination with a truly lecherous centaur-woman? Lingering pity? Or merely the pickle a boy gets in from time to time, until his time is up?

Shakespeare returned to the faltering chorus with a start. Time to trot out his boys. He hurried to the bower.

"Shall we lead the galliard, my best-best most-most lady?" wheedled Florio, the sly Italian, bowing too low.

That kind Mr. Hervey, who lived over across the downs and had recently been knighted for mysterious doings out of the country, succeeded in elbowing the fawning fellow aside. He then danced off with the lady and was followed by the lords and squires with their partners.

After the galliard came the much abbreviated play, which tripped and jingled itself to the end before his absent Lordship came baying home among his hounds and a pack of wet and hairy sailors.

Pleased murmurs and respectful laughter from the remnants of the audience as the merry young master of Tichfield plunged among the spangled players, pursuing Titania, Queen of the Fairies.

If she had been a girl, how charming would have been his enthusiasm!

Unfortunately she was Ned, sweet Mr. Shakespeare's brother, and the best Ned could do was pick up his skirts, kick off his pattens, and run like a Hampshire hog from the noble master and his howling hunters.

Still wearing his ass-head, Kemp the clown saved what was left of the night by dancing a jig and singing the latest bawdy ballad for the dwindling company. It seemed that the squires and ladies still able to move without falling down and going to sleep insisted on going home before the snowstorm got any worse.

Poor Lady Southampton-Heneage-Hervey! For the latest whisper among the country neighbours had her married to the kind Mr. Hervey, or Sir William as the flatterers remembered to call him.

"I'd do it, I swear I'd bed her and board her, if it were not for that sot of a son!"

So the kind Mr. Hervey confided to a few friends as they plodded home on their wet horses through the snow.

That last departure left the unfortunate lady prey to melancholy, dark as the deepening night.

"Sweet Mr. Shakespeare! Comfort me!"

"Dear lady, with all my heart," he answered. All that is left over, anyhow.

"Oh, he gambles so! Wastes all my substance! And ever since those horrible Danvers boys killed poor Mr. Long, who knows where murder and rape will stop?"

"It is true that order in the country is the greatest good of all," sweet Mr. Shakespeare murmured. He was thinking that perhaps the lady might go a hundred pounds. Worth trying anyhow.

"Five thousand lost at cards with the Duke of Anjou in one night!"

A hundred gained at pushpin in one night?

"Young men must live, Countess."

"Sometimes I think only you can prevail on my naughty boy, sweet Mr. Shakespeare," she whispered. Really a handsome woman, with those speaking eyes and lips . . . and that was far from all . . .

"It is youth, I think. He will be tame soon enough."

Breathing and sighing, as they whispered there in the secret room where sometimes she sheltered a priest for spiritual comfort, she leaned close and kissed him. "Such a comfort," she murmured. "I would be quite lost without you."

"All will come round in time, Countess."

"Call me Mary," she sighed. He kissed her. She kissed him

again. His kiss and her kiss melted into one long deep swooning throbbing and complete embrace.

She might even make it two hundred, he thought.

"Only you, my dear . . . only you . . ."

What was she saying? Surely not only me!

"Only you, my gentle poet . . . only you are above the sordid desires of other men . . . never would *you* stoop so low as to covet a poor widow's money . . . for now I know that you love me for myself. . . ."

chapter twelve

〰〰 DID Florio know? Had the sneaking Italian followed them? Would he whisper his latest information to Lord Burghley, or even worse, to Topcliffe the Queen's Inquisitor?

Another bed-vow broke, thought sweet Mr. Shakespeare, trudging through the snow next morning to see his company off up the river to London.

"But Willy, we need you with us! The holy justices will be after us!"

And my holy conscience is after me, he thought, waving them on their way. The dark gleaming water soon bore them out of his sight, but they remained in his mind all the rest of the week as he comforted the Countess and wrote two dozen more sonnets to her son.

"Oh, be tender! Respectful as ever, but ardent in your devotion! Chide him ever so gently, and so prevail on him that for love of you he will leave his wild companions and seek out some pure girl —"

Ever the same old theme: the wasteful boy must marry. Five thousand pounds already forfeited to the Lord Treasurer because he had refused the old man's granddaughter!

"It is our faith," the unhappy lady whispered. "Already they have torn my most devoted servants from me and embowelled them on the bloody scaffold in Holborn! My own poor Swithin, and my saintly Robert! Which of us will be next? Must I run weeping to the Queen and beg for mercy from her fierce cold heart?"

Now is the time, he thought. He whispered in her ear.

"Oh no! Poor saintly soul! In the Marshalsea?"

"We may find ways to buy her freedom. . . ."

And so that was where the money went.

As for the spoiled young lord, the admiring, loving, beseeching, chiding, scolding sonnets made him more haughty, more naughty, more reckless, more feckless, than he had been before.

Alas! I'll butter my brains, and give 'em to a dog for a New Year's gift, the disappointed poet decided.

And he packed up his few belongings and prepared to bid the pretty lordship and his winsome and willing mother farewell.

Hear me now, ye gods of flattery, fawning and fortune! Never again will this motley clown shake his bauble in the lists of flattery!

And may my barren leaves fall and rot away before some learned weevil digs 'em up and sneers: *Aha, a starveling scribbler who adored a lord! How pitiful!*

And let no limping homilies ever be made upon my sins of head or heart.

He was just about to sneak away when his Lordship caught him. "Where are the boys? Let's have that bumpkin play again."

"My Lord, I dispatched 'em to London."

"Without my will? Then fetch 'em back!"

"Your will is my will, sir."

And too great entirely, he thought, but did not say so in the peremptory presence of the giddy Earl. He had a whole clutch of secret sonnets laid away from any prying eyes, in which he laid about him soundly. In *them* there was no grovelling before the great of any sex, or lack of it. God help me if this popinjay ever finds 'em. Or his mother.

All morning he was ordered about by his Youthness and Greatness and his noble or ignoble friends, the ill-mannered Manners and the flowery Florio. Harrington the gentleman-in-waiting to the Countess also hustled him about.

Pox on this place! thought Shakespeare, smiling and bowing in all directions, so grateful in their eyes for the sunshine of their favours. Will he never throw me the money and let me go?

His Lordship gambled away three hundred pounds that evening. All his estates would be squandered in gaming and dicing. Shakespeare wrote three scolding sonnets that night, and resolved to show them to his Lordship in the morning.

It was three days before a full choir of boys good enough to play the fairies and country clowns straggled into the castle. At their head strode a famished fellow in a gaudy cloak and doublet, grinning and bowing to all lords and ladies.

Ben Jonson in another new suit!

Great squibs and rockets! thought Shakespeare. Didn't I wear that at Gray's Inn Revels in '94, when all was disorder and confusion? This cat has got into our closets!

"Well met again! Well met!" the hungry cat-man cried, licking his chops at being so near the kitchen, from which came teasing fragrance and jolly bubbling sounds.

"But Ben, but how, but who, but why —?" Shakespeare began.

"Oh, I met a fool in the forest," Jonson replied, giving him a brotherly hug. "Soft, soft, look who is with me, see who I've brought you, look, look, see there, see there," he whispered.

The slim, shy, shivering boy in the borrowed cloak was still endeavouring to conceal himself behind Robin Goffe and Nick Tooley, until young Ned himself drew him forward.

"Here's a surprise, Willy! Ben found him for you!"

The blow went right to the heart.

Wordless for once, the guilty father looked straight into the lonely eyes of his neglected son.

Ah God, the same mysterious and dreaming grey as Anne's, the same wide brow and wondering look, as of a half-wild creature hurt to the death. And how frail and wasted, from the jolly boy he had kissed a hurried goodbye on that last flight to Stratford! As Shakespeare the pampered pet of more noble ladies than he cared to remember, and not a few low wenches too, rushed toward the timid boy now hiding from him, a swarm of furious voices pursued him straight out of hell, and there was the taste of ashes in his mouth.

chapter thirteen

༝༝ "YOU ran away, father. So did I do wrong?"

"Not wrong, dear son. But worrisome to thy mother."

Hamnet said nothing to that, and tried to say nothing with his eyes. All the same, his father felt a chill of dread.

It was as though the boy were trying to tell him heavy news, and yet to spare him the blow.

"Will she not fear for thee, Hamnet?"

The boy looked innocent enough for membership in a choir of angels. And indeed the giddy Earl took a great fancy to him, and the Countess wanted him for a page.

Almost anything might have happened if a courier from young Essex had not summonded the Earl to join him at Dover with all the loose sailors he could scoop up from docks and taverns.

"Ah, happy news!" cried the giddy youth, embracing almost everybody in the house while his servants skipped back and forth with his baggage. "Oh, happy war! Our fortunes will be mended at last! Kiss me again, mother! We shall be rich!"

Shakespeare's deep eyes brightened with illumination and darkened with sadness at this renewed revelation of the real roots of these incessant wars in the name of country, honour, religion, et cetera. That old devil, money, was what all the noble words meant. Pillage of conquered towns, plunder of Spanish treasure ships, rape and slaughter in order to steal — it was hard enough for a plain old Englishman to bear the thought of all these fine people getting rich, without having to write a whole new slew of patriotic scenes full of honour, country, religion, et cetera.

It seems I am getting old, Shakespeare decided. I believed in glory before I learned it was a word like all the other words. All wind, as Ecclesiastes says. A striving after wind.

But he still wished he could dream up a way to get his hands on some of that money.

Off went the Earl at the head of a small fleet of ships, all riding high in the water because with more space below decks there would be more room for booty. Shakespeare and his little son watched the many-coloured pennons fluttering down the wind. In a week or so every boat afloat in English waters would be coming in to Dover.

Alas, why not one of mine?

Ben Jonson caught him sighing and shaking his head.

"Now what a pox is it, Will? I think I have never seen so sad a man, and with so little cause."

"We should have been shipbuilders."

"And have all our bottoms sunk? Build airy pinnaces with words, and they'll sail forever. What, man? Thou hast a son to love, a world of words to reign over, and more kingdoms to conquer. These fools of time will be tossed to oblivion ere long, but thou shalt live, and live, and live. Oh Lord, how thou shalt live! If I were a bilious man, or one given to brooding jealousy, I could look bitterly at thee, and point out thy many flaws. But not I, no, no, they could not get it out of me, it would be useless. I am too loyal."

Shakespeare perked up splendidly at that.

"What he means, he says; he's honest, we must not mind him," he whispered to his son with the big eyes, who was watching this large-voiced man in another borrowed suit as if he could not believe it.

"I like him," Hamnet whispered back.

It was true: the boy followed the ragged-haired scholar upstairs and down, in and out, around the gabled houses and barns of Tichfield, drinking in knowledge.

What a pity poor Ben's baby daughter died before she could even know him! The man was meant to amaze, startle and enlighten children. Shakespeare made his mind up instantly. We'll put old Ben in charge of the boys when we go back to London, and let him drill them in singing, dancing, fencing, speaking, running, jumping, shouting, and all according to Aristotle and fifty more authorities from antiquity.

Who knows? My own sprout may be a player yet.

Fired with hope and glory, the boy took in new life every day, and became ruddy, glowing, sparkling and merry.

All the same, his father thought, we must see what Anne says about it. He sent word through a post-horse courier that the boy was safe and well, and that they would be in Stratford together before another fortnight.

chapter fourteen

꙳꙳ AN angry Earl came stamping back to Tichfield in the dark and inmost depth of night.

"Oh, my boy! My boy! What frightful fortune hath wounded my sweet rose now?"

Everybody came bounding out in night attire to see and hear all that was woeful in the house of the poor widow now. Luckily the great lady had no male consoler with her that night, and could give full tongue to a mother's anxiety.

"Dismissed! Dismissed! Fobbed off! Pooped like a — like a prating player," sobbed his Lordship, his head in his mother's lap. "Oh, oh, all hope of glory quite, quite gone! Sent home like a truant boy, while lesser bloods than I are picked, promoted, honoured, loaded down with pomps and places! Let me die, mother, I want to die."

"Oh, speak to my boy! Cheer up his poor disordered spirits! Sweet Mr. Shakespeare, have you no words to soothe my suffering son?"

Shakespeare, in his nightgown, mustered his sleepy wits and mumbled a few noble words about honour, glory, country, et cetera, and was quite disappointed when the sweet Earl spat at him.

"And thou! Sneaking player! Parcel-poet! Take thy face off and never flatter me again! Away with you all! Take your fools' faces hence!"

When he leaped up and took a whip to them, the players decided the sweet rose of hope, et cetera, was really quite serious about disliking them.

"Thus do we see, my boy, how the twists and turns of fickle Fortune must ever be regarded in this business," Ben Jonson thoughtfully informed young Hamnet, as the players trudged through mud, over ice and through snow, on their way down to Southampton docks and their waiting barge to take them somewhere else, anywhere else.

"Indeed," Hamnet said. The word was his father's favourite.
"What did we do? Is it known?" Ned whispered.

"He will come to one or t'other of his true selves anon, of
which he has a great many, and beg us to come back," his
brother assured him.

"Well, I for one have had enough of that particular feather-
headed fool."

"It seems her Majesty sent for him to console her while her
favourite was a-plundering. The lords Derby and Mountjoy
too. Three pretty youths in place of one — it is a fair consola-
tion."

"So he will not be rich after all."

"Nor will we."

Ned straightway flung himself around on the barge in so
shocking an imitation of the hysterical Earl that all the barge-
men and loitering boobies laughed. And they cheered the
players for quite a way on their slow course up the silver
Itchen to Winchester, where they would tumble for a few
pennies at the fair, and then take post horse to London.

Every day in the smoky old city the boy seemed to draw
in more life, more hope, more light. He loved everything about
London, no matter what. The sound of his happy laughter
rang in the clacking streets, and he could not wait to greet
a new day of exciting life among these jaded, rheumy-looking,
accustomed people, who seemed not to know what wonder
waited for them around every corner.

I've needed him all this lonely time, thought the amazed
and worried father. In everything I planned for Anne and the
children I was wrong, if these few happy days can be trusted.
These fogs and damps, these pestered lanes, these noisome
ditches bearing every stench and shame of man, and even the
plagues and fires and fevers of huddled humanity — the boy
seems proof against 'em all.

But I have promised poor patient Anne, and anyhow if I'm
ever to buy that great house from Underhill the time must be
soon. For prices are going up, in this great dearth.

chapter fifteen

〽〽 SO many unwanted soldiers swarmed into the ale-houses and the pestered lanes of London that her Majesty's law-men bottled up the alehouses and drove the bad men to the streets again. So many lewd and loutish people frequented the innyards where the players were now driven to perform their undesired and unseemly shows that the constables, the beadles, the churchwardens, the vergers and all other godly and official people began shutting down innyards too, and dispersing such superfluous, vain, and shameless sinners to the suburbs, then from the suburbs to the provinces; then from the provinces back to the roads, the fields; from which unsuitable refuges the godly husbandmen and wifewomen drove them forth with hallooing and with whooping, also such barking as might be contributed by sundry snarlers and biters, low sneaking curs, hounds, mastiffs, mongrels, terriers, trindletails, dunghill dogs and bitch brachs.

"No, no, it is a sin, it denies the very dignity in a man and I will not have it for my boy," Shakespeare said, but dared not tell Hamnet yet. "A clown in motley for his father, but *he* must not be consigned to this world of dust and tinsel in which we players creep about, making fools' faces for the many-headed monster. No, no, never, never."

"Maybe so, Willy, but it will break the boy's heart," Ben Jonson said.

"Then I must leave this creeping, cringing trade and be an example of something better for him to steer his course by."

"Well, what, man, what? Name a trade, name one, name but one."

His long nose pushed forward, his little green eyes winking and flashing with intelligence, the scholar in handed-down clothes waited to pounce on any trade his famous and discontented friend might mention, and demolish it.

But it happened that an answer was just then trudging around the corner and up to the big front door of the Cross Keys, the fairest and finest inn left on the great north thoroughfare called Bishopsgate Street.

Shakespeare glanced out through the cloudy diamond window and saw the watery and glimmering light of late afternoon falling on the fat and fatuous features of a well-fed, well-clothed, and well-satisfied townsman from his own Stratford: Dick Quiney himself in the too, too solid flesh.

"A mercer," he said flatly, pushing back his chair and getting hastily up from the table.

"Thou, a fumbler of fabrics? A measurer and snipper of woven wool? A trader in the itchy threads of sheep?"

"A good fat trade, and the proof of it will be bragging before us in another little minute. For God's sake, no wild whirling words while the chief rival of my youth and reproach of my life is here. His name is Quiney and he's everything I am not, and has come to squinney at us."

"Why should we care for common men of trade?" growled Ben. "What can such knotheads know?"

"Hush, hush, take care, this is no knothead, but as shrewd a man as any I know — and he's good in Latin, too," Shakespeare muttered as Dick Quiney came striding in with arms outstretched.

"Well met, old friend!" cried the Stratford mercer, alderman and former high bailiff, advancing to embrace his cringing schoolmate. "Kind and loving greetings from the Council, and we pray you will be with us soon! How goes it? How's business? God be with us! May we be alone?"

And turning to sweep the red-headed scarecrow with a knowing glance, he added, "Give us room, good fellow, pray. I have important business with thy master."

A frightful blaze crackled up in that portion of creation in a handed-down suit now glaring from the corner.

"Dick, Dick, this is Master Benjamin Jonson, the greatest master of Latin in England, and my very good friend."

But it was already too late; the classical scholar, growling like a dog, stalked out of the inn parlour.

And Quiney was already well launched and sailing ahead on his important business, hardly hearing at all when his old schoolmate offered a comment, a demurrer, a disclaimer, or even a mutter or a mumble of doubt.

A new bishop in Worcester; many people dead in Stratford, many honest householders ruined by two great fires; much fear of war and invasion by the Spaniards; musters in the country; old Beadle Meekins dead, Tom Deege the weaver dead, and two boys dead in a week, Abe Sturley's boy Tom and Dick Woodard's boy Fulke, and many sick and impotent people to be maintained by the parish, not to speak of great building to be done all up and down High Street, and much money out at hire, ten on a hundred and very high too, but what can an honest man do? New bishop's list of stubborn property owners who would not support the parish to be drawn up and put before the Council this very week; old Catholic families on it and many new conspirers against the Crown; Tom Rogers rebuilding his fine new house after the fire and two others, too; Will Underhill's old Clopton property might be had for nearly nothing, now that the man was out of favour and on the bishop's list of stubborn Catholics . . .

His mind wandering after poor Ben Jonson, Shakespeare began to pay more attention.

"Morals down too, amongst the younkers, very bad these days," Quiney was maundering on. "Boys running off from their families, and who's to do the work if all the boys go off? Sorrow to their mothers, that is. Mistress Shagsbeer much dispirited, poor soul. Fair worried about Mistress Anne . . ."

"Ay, my boy Hamnet and I will be returning to Stratford in a few days," Shakespeare said.

"Good you can get away," Quiney said smoothly. "Yes, a good buy, a good buy if a man looked about him for a pretty property going for sixty, seventy pound, and some people in ill favour. Not all, not all. There's some sturdy citizens like your father, like Mr. Shagsbeer, may escape being on the bishop's list this time. Corn and malt that scarce, we have our worries . . ."

"What, old Deekins dead? Old Beadle dead?" Shakespeare remarked. "Sixty pounds is a bit of money for an old ruined house."

"With two barns and a toft, a good frontage on Chapel Lane, and there's stone for repair easily found, what with all the tearing down and building up," Quiney said, pouring them more sack. "A man that knows his way in the Council might find a good store of stone and a favouring will among us. If there might be interest in a good, sound old house with a long history behind it . . ."

"A haunt of conspirators in my memory," Shakespeare said. "And haunted by more than one ghost. Who would live in it? The walls look weak and the roofs and gables are warped. The old ditch that runs by the back barn all filled up. Much to be done before anyone could live in it."

"A suit by the Council coming up next week," Quiney said, "after we know who's on the list and who's off it. Lease of the Wilmcote tithes. Underhill fair going under the hill, he is, Willy. Bad blood, bad blood. That son of his, that Fulke, desperate and delinquent and might do the man harm. Sons have risen against father ere now, and will again. Last Michaelmas Term he failed his tithe rents and was presented in Chancery. For being stubborn too, after his wife died. No, a falling man, Willy, and now's the time to look at facts. If a man wants a good old property and wants to stand well and have his family stand with the Council . . ."

"A high price, Dick. Players are not in favour lately, and money is scarce. The well is stopped up too. A great lot of work to be done, but if a man might speak a word for a worthy citizen in Council, one who served the borough as chamberlain, alderman, high bailiff, and deserves well of all friends and brothers . . ."

"George Badger in trouble too. Many in trouble, with these

ruinous wars, and more war coming, we hear. What do you hear here, Willy?"

"Calais is falling, and our brave men may not arrive in time to catch it. Old Beadle dead! No plague this summer in Stratford?"

"Drains all bad and barns all low in malt and corn. Who keeps it? Who is holding out? That old application for a coat of arms, Willy, never came to good. All of us had our arms from Heralds' College these twenty years, but old John Shagsburr's always held back. Stubborn in religion, in those days. But might be off it this time . . ."

So it went on, around and around, back and forth, evasion upon evasion, and hint upon hint, although no threats seemed to be made.

"A man might sue for you with Underhill at a shrewd time, Willy, if so disposed . . ."

"I might find the money, though players are out of favour . . ."

"Too bad you didn't take up where your father left off, many people say. Oh, Gilly and Richie were comfort of sorts, until Gilly went into hats, and Richie went with Smith. Leaves the old man without a son to back him up, and that's bad . . ."

"Would ten pounds now be any help?"

"He might look at twenty."

At last they made the deal and shook hands. Quiney rose, embraced him again, and departed for more important business.

Shakespeare saw him out, and then went looking for Ben Jonson.

chapter sixteen

SO it was decided, and still the boy did not know.

I'll make it up to him, if I never do anything else, Shakespeare thought. Trade in half my shares with the Burbages, go see Garter King at Arms and pay him thirty pounds, then ride to Stratford for the summer.

He watched young Hamnet going through his daily training with old Ben, and felt like a murderer.

"Ah, that's it, stride, squat, jump and turn. Round three times, feint, feint, feint! Kill not your man yet, tease him a little on, make him come on the blade, and thrust! To the heart! Ah, good boy. Very good. Is he not good, Will?"

Shakespeare agreed that Hamnet was very good at fencing, at dancing, at singing, at leaping, jigging, marching, at shouting and at whispering, good in all things necessary to make a player.

"Ah, and when he takes the fainting, simpering, bashful parts, and plays the country milkmaid, he'll have the galleries in a roar," Ben said, beaming.

"Oh, he's good at it, the boy is very good."

The boy beamed too; he was blooming.

Next day the sneaking stepson of Justice Gardiner served the Lord Chamberlain's Men with a writ of prohibition against the performance of any more stage plays in Southwark, likewise in all Surrey. Now Fate has done the murder for me, Shakespeare thought, and was glad he had traded in half his shares in the sinking company, and only just in time.

The money for Underhill, if he'll take it. The money for our coat of arms. And money enough to tide us over until the autumn. Who knows? I might indeed take up my father's business and be at last a man of substance in the town.

He told Hamnet.

107

And in three days they rode together on hired post horses out of the teeming city and took the broad new road past St. Giles's in the Fields.

Lord, have mercy on us, someone had scrawled on a crumbling wall.

The ancient prayer, good against the plague, or nearly anything.

The postboy chirrupped and sang stray catches and new murder ballads, and there were three stout mercers riding with them to Oxford.

Then onward through green fields into Warwickshire, while the quiet son hardly gave a sign that he had been stricken to the heart.

When they came in sight of the old Hathaway homestead, Shakespeare began to tremble. Alas that Anne had taken the children and moved back in with old Dame Hathaway! He let the post horses drink a long while at the little brook. Then slowly he and Hamnet rode on.

Judy was feeding a kitten in the yard. They could see its pink tongue making wrinkles in the milk. The horses' hoofs made no sound in the lush wet grass, but the creak of the saddle caused her to look up. And then too, Hamnet coughed.

"Judy, here's your brother!"

She retreated, keeping an eye on them, her freckled face screwed up tight. Then she turned and ran for the house, and when she reached it, turned again. Her pale eyes were round, her mouth was open. She was eyeing the horse, the bulging saddlebags.

A moment more and her reedy figure, topped by straggling reddish locks, had disappeared. Soon a strange young girl came to the kitchen door and peered out. It was Susie, madly grown, like a mocking puppet of herself, a stretched-out child on long bandy legs.

"Susie, I've a new gown for thee!"

Susie came slowly forward. She looked anxiously at Hamnet, then ran forward and held up her hands to help him down.

"Did he get sick?" she asked.

"No, no, he's well, he's the bravest of the brave, a bawcock, a boy of gold!"

Shakespeare heard his hypocritical words echoing back at him from the mossy trees, the dripping thatch-eaves, the viney walls.

"Poor Hamnet," Susanna said, kissing him tenderly and already too cheerful, like all well people in the endless conspiracy against the sick and doomed.

"I've presents from London, and we're hungry, Susie," the father said.

"I'm not hungry," said Hamnet.

Her wise and knowing glance flickered to her father's face and they were at one in the conspiracy, if in nothing else.

Exile, he thought. From myself and now from my own. The truth creeps in like my old dog Crab, with that old bone mortality in his mouth. The boy must know.

Coldness, as of death itself, fingered his very bones. He shivered as he followed them into the dark and chilly cottage of the Hathaways, now the last refuge for his wife and children. And loathing, deeper and darker than any he had ever known in the darkest night ever yet suffered by his soul, now made its home in his inmost and secret self, where slimy shapes crawled in darkness, and idiot gibbering between one fool and another, all wearing his own features, ran on and on in his weary brain.

But no! It was the steady drone of an ill-remembered, a fatally futile voice, mumbling the same mournful messages: old lady Hathaway, not even Anne's mother and so a doubly-stepped grandmother to the tolerated and not even secretly resented children. As soon as the haunted father stooped to enter at that low, stained doorway, and inhaled the mouldy air of this home that was never home, he knew they must all escape from this plague upon the hearth, this stooped and sagging figure by the feeble fire, whose eternal voice went croaking on, and on, and on.

"Ah! So it is thee, Willy Shagspear. Brought him back again, I see. Your wife is sick. Never been the same since the child-bed fever when she lost the last one, and her husband away . . ."

"Where is she? Where is my Anne?"

"Upstairs," murmured Susie beside him. Great God, the girl is protecting me already. And he felt the first warm wave of tenderness return to him in this desert of self-loathing.

He reached desperately for her darling hand, and felt strength surge back into his soul.

Old New Place, he thought, and wanted to cry for joy. I'll go see Mr. Underhill in the morning, and prevail on him to let 'em live in the house even before we have the money to buy it.

The endless lamentation of Dame Hathaway followed them up the crooked, dark, and narrow stairs.

Why, she's my own Susie still, he thought, and the uneven shapes of the stairs moved crazily in a glimmer of tears.

At the landing, he took her sweet freckled face gently in his hands and kissed her. The girl smiled at him, patted his hands, and hurried down to the kitchen to bring Hamnet to his mother. He saw and felt and knew with all his heart the young girl's eager solicitude for the little brother who had never been strong, who had always needed protection.

The door to the small room over the kitchen was open a little. He felt the trembling in his whole body as he opened it and went softly in.

The room was dark; the shutters were closed. At first he did not see the shadowy figure lying in the rude, small bed.

"Anne?"

When she made no sound, he went forward softly, so that he could look down at her.

She lay among pillows, the dim oval of her face shadowed with long hair; she lay with her head resting on one arm, as she always did in sleep. Bending closer, he heard her slow breathing. And then he saw her eyes, wide open, looking at him.

"Oh, my love, my wife . . ."

A heavy sigh came from her, and a faint moaning sound, as of weariness or despair. She did not speak, but went on looking at him, without moving.

For a moment, as he waited, feeling a light shiver go through him, the whole dark room seemed mutely telling of things hidden there: the hangings, the dim corners, the silent figure in the bed, all gave him his answer; and the heavy air grew clamorous with reproach, and tremulous with swarming fears.

He ran to the shutters, flung them open; and a grey light crept into the room. Then he turned and faced her.

The harsh light showed him how thin and pale she had become, how wasted as though by fever, the grey eyes in deep hollows now, and unspeakably sad.

She trembled violently as he looked at her, and then pressed her hands to her face and sobbed.

The squawking of old lady Hathaway came nearer, nearer, and now she was in the room and her words went on and on in an unending stream. "There you see what you've done to her, Willy Shakespeare . . . fie, fie, fie . . . mallicholly she is with sorrow at her sad fate, wife of a forbidden player . . . warned her I did. . . . John Pace would ha' married her, and the best bottoms in the county, and a barn full of corn and malt. . . . No, she would not, too good for a good stout man and churchgoer. . . . You'll make your bed, I said, and you'll come to lie in it, you will, mark my words . . . but did she hear? Had a cough she did, and the failing, and the falling sickness, and the cramp, and the convulsion of the mouth, and the distemper and the sweating, and the fever, and what did he do? Did he so much as send to inquire of his wife he married and left to the charity of his fine family? No, that he did not, nor his children either, poor souls, left without their father, naked to the winds if them with a heart, and a Christom charity, hadna given her a home, and much gratitude from him there's ever been, no, nor money either. . . ."

Great howling spirits of the air, how long has this been, and when shall it have a stop?

He took his poor weeping wife in his arms, and they wept together. Ages passed and the shrewish dame continued her remarks. Hamnet ran in and joined his suffering parents, and so did the two daughters, and finally they were all huddled together, like exiles in an unfriendly country, managing to mutter a little to one another, nod, smile, sigh, make a few faces, shrug, and at the last, to speak rationally and make some sense in the surrounding madness of sheer word-broth.

Alas, my poor chicks and their hen, he thought. I must find them shelter at once, or take them all back to London, plague or no plague, constables or no constables. Nothing can be worse than this. And they say *I* talk too much. They say once started that *I* sometimes have to be stopped.

Let them hear this, let them hear this. But may some friendly fairy stop up his bunghole before it quite floods the world.

Melancholy, forsooth! Of course my poor, sweet, patient Anne is melancholy. With a forbidden player for husband, with a dark and smoky house to cower in from the never-ending rains, and with this shrew of all shrews to people the mind with gibbering idiot histories, why would she not run right straight out of her mind, and never want it back again?

Oh, I have been blind, deaf and selfish. Oh, I have been a poor wordy fool. But now I must act. Now I must bring off the greatest deed of my poor forbidden dusty life.

I'll to my father first, and to Dick Quiney second, and to Mr. Underhill third. This town shall see at last that all these years I've had my plans, and my dreams, and all of them for

my patient, my saintly, my incomparable wife and my astonishing children. All with eyes, ears, noses, organs, and the gift
of eating, drinking, speaking, and dancing and laughing too,
if the talking engine will ever stop.

But old John Shakespeare had let the western house for such
storage space as could still be used after the fire. The back
house was rented to the Badgers. No room, no room, all
crowded into one narrow little house now, and how long,
Willy, how long before you provide a house yourself?

"You'll see, father, you'll see. . . ."

Dick Quiney twiddled his thumbs, coughed discreetly, tiptoed to the door, closed it softly, tiptoed back, and whispered
in his old schoolmate's ear.

"What, Lady Jocosa says not?"

"Hush, Willy, hush . . . little trouble there you know . . .
irregular in religion . . ."

"But if Underhill would sell, then why must she have further say?"

"In the bond, Willy, in the bond. Perhaps a word with you,
eh? The lady is full of flights and fidgets, always was you
know . . . a calming word perhaps, from one she ever looked
with favour on . . ."

"Favour? On me? Not that I know of . . ."

But he rode off to see Lady Jocosa, anyhow, and found the
handsome and high-spirited lady very fretful. It took a whole
afternoon to bring up the subject, and then when it was up,
a whole evening to get her off it. The answer was no, no, no,
and that was her last irrevocable word. Unless she could ex-
pect him tomorrow afternoon again, to bring it up some
more? And the afternoon after that, and a whole flock and
flapping of long afternoons, sweet Willy, the most perfect
player and the hardest-hearted man who ever had scorned a
merry, madcap, ever-willing lady in all history — well, Willy?
Well?

If Anne ever knew what ends I must meet, and what

lengths I must go to, in this world pestered with concupiscent wenches, she would not want to live in the biggest and finest house I could buy for her with soul, body and money. How long, how long?

chapter seventeen

ༀༀ "ALAS, these terrible long cold rains! They pierce my walls, be they never so thick!"

The voice of old Mrs. Hathaway nagging, nagging at them, even in sleep.

And how to sleep in the Hathaway house, under these smoky rafters, with all his regrets and fears swarming about him for company? So much time gone from him already, and so much of it wasted! What had he done in all these years to justify his craven flight from Stratford? What had he accomplished that would justify his abandonment of Anne and his children? He had ached and shivered and starved in a few attics, feasted at other people's banquets, flattered a few pompous fools, heard and spoken many windy words, and written far too many of his own. Which of all his little triumphs would satisfy Anne for her lonely years of waiting? An overwhelming tide of compassion and regret surged over him. How many times had he returned to Stratford since his flight? Alas, those visits were easily tallied. It had been nearly a year since the last one. He was so humiliated that he could not bestow even the compliment of curses upon himself.

So it was that his tremendous resolve was born to atone, as well as he was able, to the terribly changed woman he had, after all, married.

Never the same since her fever after the fire last September. "Worked so hard to save other people's houses, and never a house for her own poor children," Dame Hathaway informed him. But she more than informed him about everything. "All the south side of Sheep Street, gone. All the east side of High Street, gone. All the south side of Bridge Street, that's gone. Tom Ward, Nick Barnhurst, George Badger, all lost, all burned to the ground. And your fine friends Hamnet and Judith Sadler lost their shop, in spite of my daughter slaving and

115

digging and getting sick for her pains. And was there any gratitude? Did any of her fine friends so much as throw her a thank you? Lying on her bed of pain, poor girl, with no husband to hold her head or pay her way, and who of the fine Shagspears came to her rescue then? Did John Shagspear, that talked so big and walked so fine all the years of his pride and now is fallen like us all into dust and darkness? Oh, the Lord and his vengeance are heavy, and the days of his darkness shall be many. What does the Good Book say? The Crown Inn destroyed too. The Bear is all dust and ashes. There's your lesson for drinking with your fine friends. But will they listen? Will they learn? They have ears and eyes, but will they hear? Will they see?"

Great God, what a wonder old lady Hathaway's husband had not died in despair on his wedding night! Wretched fellow, to have climbed into bed beside that talking curse every night for twenty-five miserable years — wretched, wretched fellow! Oh, alas, poor Dick, now I know why he died every day, and never knew a peaceful night! It took a long time, but at last it killed him.

"Now Anne, why didst not marry John Falk before he tired of thee, who has two horses, and a fine house unburnt, and the best pigs and bottoms, ay, and sheepfolds too, and barns, all free and clear, instead of this walking sorrow, a player who'll be hounded out of the parish yet, mark my words. . . . Why didst bring this sorrow on me, a widow with no means of protection? And Hamnet that thin and pale and never eats, come home with a fever again in all this snow and ice and wet weather! Heartbroken he is at his father wandering the roads with his fine friends, the scum of the roads I say, and you'll hear it in church too, to my shame. . . ."

When the boy is well again I'll take him to London, the guilty wanderer thought. What a prince he could play! Far truer by nature than many of these princelings I have seen at Court, with their stolen lands and manors!

As if in compensation for the eternal muttering of the old

lady, the mortal boy attempted to cheer his father in any way he knew.

"Is it the headache, father?" Hamnet would whisper, while his small hand sought the place that hurt, to smooth the pain away. "I'll hold your head any time, father. I'll sit all the night and watch by you. I'll be quiet as a mouse."

Alas, he tried to escape, even as I did twenty years ago, the regretful father thought. If one of the Queen's pressmen had seen my boy he'd have been snatched up for the Chapel Choir, or Paul's. Or even our own company, God forbid.

So frail, so gentle it frightens me. Not wild and wanton like me. I think there was never such a gracious creature born.

How wonderfully constructed he was, like a boy on a Greek urn, and yet English in everything!

When he is well again . . . when he is well . . .

As for the two daughters, they skipped about and chattered all day long. Judith especially, who seemed to have absorbed vigour as fast as her twin brother had lost it. They were so noisy that Anne, roused sometimes from her feverish dreams, would cry out at them to be quiet, and then sink into apathy again.

The insane structure of this life in which the poor player wandered like a stranger seemed any time now to be going to topple with all its unreal people and his dreams of them, leaving him in the ruins.

His mother, too, was spinning dreams of the days to come or the days that never were. Religion to Mary Shakespeare had become the last road to felicity or madness, he could not tell which.

"Mother, I serve the Queen and cannot listen to these dreams of yours. . . ."

"Only wait, only wait till the great day of wrath!"

"Mother, why did Anne leave our house? In only a little while I'm buying one, and then we'll see . . ."

Old John Shagspear, sunk in dark gloom, brooded over the debts he owed and the tithes he would not pay to these prying surveyors and overseers in the name of one bishop or t'other.

"Never!" he would growl, lifting a meaty fist and subsiding into dark grudges and countergrudges again. Gilly was very big indeed, running his own hat-shop. Richie was a patient drudge.

"Ay, and where are the best ones? Where is my Will, and where is little Ned? Run after the plays they have, and wasted their brains away. Those are the two my hopes were for. Those are the ones that might have saved us from the bishops and the sneaking scriveners. Ay, and the damned Puritans, Will. They drove me out of the Corporation, and now they want my last bit of property, hounded by debt as I am, I who have been alderman in this borough, and affeeror, and chief bailiff, and chamberlain, and not even a coat of arms to say I'm a man of substance. What is my substance? A shadow. What are we all in this life? That damned Lucy, that damned lousy Lucy has been saying you stole a deer from Charlecote —"

"But he's said that of every boy in town, father. It is the fat man's thin jest."

"Alas, my hopes! Alas, my dreams!"

So he found his people, after his long freedom.

And old Crab the dog eyed him sourly from the chimney corner, as if he smelled of all-too-human sins.

But he left the house with reluctance all the same, feeling like a guest who had stayed too late. They saw him politely to the door; they wished him a kind good night, while huddling companionably together and waiting for him to go; and then, peering disconsolately through the window, he saw them hurry eagerly back to their snug hearth again.

He waded home through rain and splashed through mud and water, back to his wife.

It was a month of rains. Clouds lowered in the sky all of the time, and the wind seemed never still: sifting through the cracks in the windows, rattling the leaded panes sharply, swooping down the chimney and smothering the feeble fire, penetrating the thickest garments, making the family shiver even in their beds.

And Dame Hathaway's temper did not improve. When the chill wind nipped her ears and empurpled her nose, her voice came from blue lips with a keener edge. The eyes seemed congealed in that frigid flat countenance; the bony elbows appeared harder and sharper than icicles; her figure looked as though if it ever bent it would snap with a loud metallic sound. He kept away from her. Oh, so carefully, he kept away from her. He did not wish to be petrified in that arctic glance; it was cold enough without any chill emanations from her.

So April ended and a mouldy May came dankly and drearily to mock their hopes of warmth and sunshine.

Great Jupiter Pluvius! Would England always drip?

With leaden legs and batty eyes he plodded about this cankered, rheumy shire, where the green wheat rotted and the fold stood empty in the drowned field, and all was mouldy, reeking in the immortal fog and the river's breath.

"Peas and beans are as dank here as a dog," said old Will Greenway the Stratford carrier. "Things are not the same since the old Earl died."

"Not the same. Nay, not the same."

While the goodmen wagged their beards and old Dame Hathaway talked, the restless Shakespeare muttered with certain friends in markets and odd places about the shire.

Three wet summers now, and a dearth of wheat and barley. John Combe, Tom Russell, Ad Quiney said they'd have a go at it, if he would take all the risk.

"Very well."

"Ten in the hundred for me," said John Combe.

Shakespeare shrugged, and they all shook hands. After a cup of sack together they went their ways.

Three weeks later the Stratford Corporation enjoined all

citizens from engrossing and forestalling of grain, for the short-
age now was very great. Who could have cornered the market
in corn and malt?

Shakespeare did not tell the aldermen, neither did he inform
the burgesses, and anyhow he had become subject to long fits
of abstraction, forgetting to answer when anyone spoke.

One day he told Anne that he was leaving for London soon.
She said nothing against it, but Mistress Hathaway said everything.

"Now hear what I say!"

Ages passed; the sun and the stars rolled on their courses;
many people died; many were born; and there was no end
to the things happening all over the world. Mistress Hathaway
went on talking.

It was late when they went to bed that night. In the morning, refreshed, she began once more to tell her thoughts. For
breakfast they had porridge and milk, and talk, and for dinner
cabbage and beans, and talk; but neither he nor Anne wanted
any supper. Silent, they remained by the hearth, while her
discourse swept over and above and around them, filling the
dark house with a never-ending vociferation.

They would sleep, though; they would sometimes fall into
a sodden and fretful sleep, cringing in their beds.

One morning he sat up, shivering, and listened for the
wordy curse to fall upon them again. Only the rain, murmur-
ing a disconsolate threnody to the eaves; but he thought Anne
had been weeping beside him, in the darkness of night and
loneliness.

Blessed be God, the poor wan woman was sleeping.

Hear me now, sprites of the air, all ye hobgoblins and
winged messengers of the powers of darkness. . . .

And he renewed his solemn vows to atone, to be a success,
to make everybody proud, everybody with eyes and ears and
memories, of that badgered and beaten thing like a thing like
a man, Willy the Spearshaker of Stratford.

Tomorrow, no, today I go to Underhill of Idlicote and put it to him, ay or no. Lady Jocosa and all wagtail wenches from here to Timbuctoo may henceforth whistle the wind for me, yea, verily, and all old shrews too, all clapper-tongued hags from here to . . .

Hark! Was she up and at it again?

A snore came from the misery chamber where the old woman slept and gained strength for another dreadful day.

He lay down and grappled with his swarming fears and apprehensions until sweet goddess Sleep crowned him with her garland. . . .

A bell tolled faintly, and was still. Again. Behind grey dripping hazel bushes the mutes set down their load. Someone was dead, lying behind the dim hazel bushes in her coffin, on which the rain tapped and tapped, a heavy hollow sound. . . . His mother-in-law. What? Was Mistress Hathaway dead? What? Was Mistress Hathaway dead? But no — it was not the rain tapping — it was she; and at the sound the mutes gave a look at one another, and the mutes walked rapidly away. Tap, went her knuckles, demanding her rights; and then her eyes were glowering under the lid for someone to blame for all this; tap, tap — and she had her head out, and her hands out, and her arms out, and her shoulders out, and now she was climbing out of the coffin and making for the guiltiest and most degraded wretch in the universe —

Ah yes, me.

He sat up in bed, holding his aching head.

How, how, how?

See Underhill today. Tell him we must, we must. Send a boy to Jocosa and tell her . . . tell her . . .

Stay away forever, forever, ay, forever from jumping Jocosa.

The insatiability of fine wenches should be advertised abroad. The world should hear about our high and mighty ladies, of such lust that apes and monkeys would goggle at it. Ay, and centaurs, and alley cats.

Well, well, when I get back to London with the door locked I shall cause three or four new wenches to leap forth in all their lechery. But will the world thank me for lifting their skirts so high? One way to smother their never-ending voices, anyhow.

But the voice of Lady Jocosa would not be smothered so easily. Through the dripping lanes it laughed at him all the way to Fillongley, where old Underhill lived his little dry life, still mourning his dear departed Mary and letting his rough boys run wild.

"I asked for you in Idlicote, sir," Shakespeare told this narrow grey man, who seemed all made of fear. He had been knocking, knocking at the rich man's narrow gate for many minutes before the grating was drawn back and a veiny eye peeped out.

"Ask for me not at Idlicote, nor anywhere my enemies can spy me out. Ask for me nowhere," whined the unhappy widower, starting to close the grating.

"But sir, the big house! New Place! I'm ready to execute the bond and move in with my wife —"

"Bad times, bad times, we're all in their bad books," came the quavering voice. "Your father too, they have him written down with me. We cannot move this year."

"All repairs I'll take on myself, Mr. Underhill!"

As his voice waxed, old man Underhill's waned.

"Come back next year, next year —"

"Lady Jocosa! Lady Jocosa promised me!"

A thin reedy laugh, or was it a sob? No matter. The mourning man was gone.

As Shakespeare mounted his father's wet horse he heard another voice raised in angry disputation inside the house.

That would be young Fulke, the idiot and epileptic heir.

"Kill! Kill! I'll k-k-kill you!"

And so he may, thought the weary husband and three-times father as he rode back all those muddy miles to his own hiding place, under Dame Hathaway's dripping eaves.

Murder in all his ugly forms leered, crept, sprang and struck down his victims at every turn in the road. Murder leaped out at him from every dark and secret convolution of his brain.

He stopped in the High Street before his old friend Phil Rogers' apothecary shop.

Or pepper and spice shop, really, with only a dark corner given over to that ill trade in pills and poisons.

Cold, wet, muddy and aching all over, he stood there in this dusty and furtive place, breathing as little as possible. I made my apothecary in this borrowed likeness, he thought, as Philip Rogers peeped and squinted at him over his German spectacles. Dry shards of tattered hair hung down on either side of Philip's lean and leathery nose. Bad teeth, poor eyes, and shaking hands, and his breath might have issued from a peat bog.

"Alas, Willy, they persecute an innocent man. What have I ever done? There's no profit in these poor herbs and salts. A little tobacco, or I know not what would become of me with all this persecution. How's things in London?"

"Better, I hope, this year," murmured his old friend sadly. Let him but wail me a few bars more, and I'll be down in the dumps with borrowed woe. "Philip, my wife needs a doctor."

"I bled her myself," Philip moaned. "Bled her good, and sold her three decoctions and my best confection of atropine and rose hips. Her mother is never satisfied, and owes me yet. Ten shillings and tuppence it is. A bad winter and a bad spring."

"I'll pay you today," said the muddy visitor. "Or no, it had better be tomorrow. I had forgot Dame Hathaway needs pitch and a roll of lead. What of that new physician from Paris I heard was coming here?"

"Your father had Earl Ambrose's own man, Willy, from Warwick. Alligators' eyes! Toads' livers! Very expensive. Never did her good, poor woman."

Shakespeare was getting the aches now in his stomach as well as in his legs and in his head.

"I'll tell you a secret, Willy," whispered Philip, beckoning him forward. A breath as from a charnel house.

"That new preacher," whispered the unhappy apothecary, "put the fears of hell and eternal burning into that girl. I heard him. Said that to lie with you and not get children was the unforgivable sin. Laid the fear of fire and burning on her poor lonely soul. And the Council forbade all plays in the borough and set the dogs on 'em. She dreams of dogs and devils, Willy. Tearing her sweet white flesh, and rending you too, she told me when the old woman was not listening. . . ."

Shakespeare felt his skin crawling and his stomach turning. He absently shook hands with his whimpering friend and rode back to Shottery in the rain.

Crowded into a tight pew in Holy Trinity Church, that Sunday, the base husband and treble father gave his usual imitation of an interested listener as the loud and learned Mr. Barton blew himself up and discharged a windy sermon upon the congregation.

"Oh, my good people, what is the will of the Lord? What hath He in store for those who would divine His intentions? We cry unto Him for succor in this unending dearth, this cold, this rain, when the skies do lower and the sun and moon wax dim, and our hearts do faint with fear and our stomachs with hunger. Our July hath been like to a February, our June even as an April, our years are turned upside down, our summers are no summers, our harvests are no harvests. For a long and weary space of time scant any day hath been seen that it hath not rained upon us. Now why and how hath this dreadful trial descended upon us, the Faithful of the Lord?"

In the ringing stillness the hot-eyed preacher leaned down to stare from face to face.

"Oh, my children, do ye ask why? Do ye dare ask how and why of the God of Heaven?"

No answer from the well-washed people of the congregation.

Sadly the voice of Mr. Barton came, sadly the head of Mr. Barton shook.

"Shall we not look inward and see that it is our sins? Yea, our grievous, our shameful sins that have so grieved our Lord that He hath hidden His countenance from us? Ah, until we repent and alter our sinful ways, have we not learned that no sun of grace shall shine, no blessing shall be given?"

Shakespeare caught Dame Hathaway's accusing eye upon him, and lost his place in the hymnal.

Pray God none of these custodians of virtue reads my creeping mind.

How fortunate that all my priests and nuns are either French or Italian, and safe from these vengeful Protestants in the dusty files of Time!

As the subdued flock huddled there in the harsh glare from the eye of righteousness, their faces bathed in the unlovely light from the plain glass windows, he closed his eyes and tried to return to those happy childhood days when the saints, the angels, the purple and crimson and the heavenly blue of old stained glass bathed the faces of the people, and the noble music of Latin spoke not to the doubting mind, but to the humble soul.

chapter eighteen

❧❧ HAIL to thee sweete Willie in thy home of countrie pleasures. Much has transpired since thy going. Thy hungry frend Ben Johnson hath been remooved bodilie once more by Old Man Henslowe to make goode hys brag that hee can write a beter plaie than anie man now extante includinge thee. And thys weeke the Admiralls Men begin their horrible rehearsings of The Ile of Dogs whyche Ben has broughte fouthe wyth muche groaninge & wonderful boasts.

As for thy fellowes wee muste have twoe newe plaies at once to grab a harveste of pennies befor the privie council forbidds us agayne on acct of Plague thys sommer. Helpe us Willie wyth two lustie plaies of War Deathe Bloode & Riot I smell it on the ayre for the people are restless wyth all thys dearth of rye & corn and constant impressing of men into the army. Easter Sunday they did lock the churches in all London untill the presters did take up 1000 men from divine sarvice. A man myt go for to loose hys religion.

Come to us if thou canst in Faversham where the ships are bilding & the trained bandes are drillinge. Doo not fayle us sweet Chucke. At the Bell in Faversham.

Richd Burbadge

Deliver to Mr. William Shakspre in Stretford-on-Affon

War! Blood! Riot! Carnage! Gore! Gore!

The suddenly happy Shakespeare sniffed the breeze and found it coming from south-southeast. Very good.

"My fellows need me at once, and I must go," he said to Anne.

A joy almost hidden from him immediately, but there all the same, shone briefly from her eyes.

That gives me my answer, and it seems the only one possible, he thought.

126

"I'll go with thee, father!"

Alas, the boy had heard.

"Oh, I would die," Anne said. "That terrible London, where so many die of plague. I would never sleep or rest."

"No, it is not London, it is the salubrious seashore. It is the health resort of Faversham, in Sussex. All the best people go there. And I shall return before the summer begins. I promise."

"Oh, but he is not strong, his poor lungs are weak —"

"My fellows need me only to scratch off two little plays. I have 'em all in my head. It would do the boy good."

"And I know them, they may need me too, I can help them too," Hamnet said. He was quivering all over like a race horse.

The dark and direful lamentations of Dame Hathaway pursued them out of Stratford and onto the highroad. They rode always with other travellers, well-armed, for there was more murder and robbery on the highways in this year of dearth than had been known in living memory. Hamnet rode a new roan, while his father bestrode a powerful bay. And both of them sang.

Snug and warm in the host's own parlour at the Crown, in the goodly city of Oxford, they supped on a spiced haunch of venison with mustard. And for merry companionship they had the rosy hostess herself, who fell instantly in love with Hamnet.

"So like his father! Such a man already! With a fair and heart-breaking eye! And oh Lord, what a leg!"

Shakespeare was feeling a little queasy.

She has not changed, he thought. "We had better ride on to Sanford for the night," he remarked between admiring and affectionate speeches from the sportive Jane, whose husband, old John Davenant, had the sciatica.

"Why, father? We're so jolly and warm right here!"

"Oh, cruel and stubborn man! He would take his poor horses and his darling son out into that cold rain! Is our house not warm? Is our food not good? Is our fire not hot? Are our beds not soft? Oh, I'll take it hard, I will!"

The haunted husband and frustrated father put on his hat and cloak. He took seven, eight, nine, ten steps to the door. He opened it to the cold rain and the whimpering wind. Hamnet regretfully wrapped himself in his own cloak and pulled the hood over his ears.

"Oh, they surely will not go out in such a tempest!"

"Why, dear father? Why?"

"We have twenty mile to go tonight before we sleep. I have decided to ride to Redington."

"To Redington! The man has taken leave of his senses!" moaned Mrs. Davenant.

"Be certain, you never spoke truer words," said the haunted husband, splashing toward the stable across the innyard, with his son splashing after him, still asking why.

Happy with hay and oats in the stable of the Crown, the two innocent horses munching and crunching.

"Ye're not going out in that storm, master?" said the ostler.

Shakespeare looked at Gog, the big bay, and at Magog, the young roan. He looked at his little son, and could not meet his eyes. Virtue itself turns vice, being misapplied, he thought.

And having thus lulled in the wild sea of his conscience for a little while, he said good night to the ostler, patted the two horses' necks, took Hamnet by the hand, and splashed back to the warm, snug, merry parlour, where the hostess served them both spiced ale, in full forgiveness.

Some rather teasing moral thoughts did indeed occur to him during the night, and he resolved to remember them later, when he could put them in a play. Everything in its place, to make a long story short.

While Hamnet slept in the truckle bed with the hostess's little son, and while Mr. Davenant slept with his sciatica, it was possible that Shakespeare slept with the hostess; but if so, it was long, snug, warm, and happy hours later.

"Can we lie with them again, father?" the happy Hamnet

asked, the minute they were mounted and clop-clopping away from the ancient city of rusty towers and spires, chiming steeples and twittering trees, following the winding river beyond the bridge and so on among the Chiltern Hills, beneath a marvellously untidy sky, all broken and scattered clouds.

Shakespeare woke up and knew not where he was, or why.

"Father? Why are you sleeping *now*, father?"

A good thing he was awake. The nineteenth or twentieth band of pressed men, the scum of the hills, idlers, wanderers, vagabonds, driven cursing past them by two sergeants in buckram suits, with a watchful bailiff riding after them, to pick off any rogue who made a dash for freedom.

"It is a way I sometimes travel," the father explained to his son.

"Can we lie with them again, father? Oh, how we laughed, Rob and I! Woke up and laughed, slept again, and laughed. If we lived here and I went to the University we could sleep with them again. Could we, do you think, father?"

Shakespeare was dozing off again. The best way to avoid guilty thoughts.

A company of Cotswald farmers, mercers and hog butchers caught up with them, and for a little way through the green vales and the budding orchards they rode with this company.

"A fine day. The rain may end. Mould and rot will ruin us else. Your boy, master?"

Shakespeare fought through the haze of sleep, the wrack of remorse, and agreed that this was his boy.

"A fine boy, young to be on the roads. In times like these."

"He loves it, as you can see, sir."

"Not in school, I see that though."

"He finished early, earlier than I did. I was not much of a one for school, myself, either."

"No more was I, master. A long, long time, learning all that stuff to unlearn later."

Shakespeare was falling asleep with this dull conversation. Another ragged band of pressed men cursed their leaders too loudly and woke him again.

But no, it was the bleating of a flock of sheep.

Onward they rode, and onward through the green heart of England.

Shakespeare had buried his thoughts of the generous Jane beneath a handy blanket of anxiety over writing any more plays about war.

Oh God, how I hate the noise and smoke and stink of it! How can I fool the people with my trumpets and excursions when so many of them will be meeting the fire-eyed goddess face to face? Oh, what a rogue and peasant slave am I! Never to have written out of my own petty life, but always out of dusty books and patched old plays! Why is it that someone has not found me out?

The fiery locks and pocky cheeks of Ben Jonson floated out of the dismal swamp of his mind. Ah, there's an honest man, who could anatomize my weaknesses one by one, and do me the good I need. Pray God he scapes the hunters, and we meet again soon. Hamnet likes him too. Alas, that we are such faulty fathers, when any poor shepherd would rank higher in his parenthood! Well, I will have that house for Anne if I must go to Lady Jocosa again and —

It is true that some day I must grapple with my weakness, which is, I fear, getting stronger than ever.

Well, if I must have one, it is better that it should be women, than that it should be some other things. Like money, or too much drinking. Every man must have his weakness, and it is well that I know what mine is.

The future began to look interesting, considered in the light of battles still to come with unknown daughters of our unlucky mother, Eve.

If we meet many more bands of vagabonds who must be soldiers, my weak interest in war will quite fade away before I have written his bloody plays for my poor trusting partner. I wonder if I can fob him off with a merry comedy about a money-lending Jew. And perhaps Tom Kyd's old *Hamlet*, pieced out with what I've learned from Montaigne and Francis Bacon, to make a good bloody tragedy for the people and a tortured war of will and conscience, for the queasy ones who read and think too much.

We'll see. Some few scores of miles more, and we'll see.

But I'm glad that now I know my weakness, and can fight it all the way across England, and back, if so it should be necessary.

chapter nineteen

꧁꧂ THE reunited partners had barely had time to shake hands and embrace before splitting again.

"What I thought, Dick, was that I could dress up our old *Hamlet* play in new clothing, add some drums and trumpets, some good new murders, a little more passion than I gave you for Romeo, and —"

"Our mouldy *Hamlet* again! Give me no more passion than Romeo and I'll keep myself well cooled with my own wind. *Hamlet,* forsooth! I said war! I said blood! I said —"

Young Hamnet beheld this brawl with both eyes and heard it with both ears. He seemed fascinated with such recklessness in any man who would so noisily disagree with his father.

All the fatigues and pains, the monotonies and burdens of their journey were already beginning to fade, now that they were here at the very mouth of the Swash, inhaling the salubrious fragrance of oakum, pitch, tar, and above all, the mighty sea-smell itself. Now his father was talking, quietly and reasonably.

"We must remember, Dick, that my last two tries at bloody war got us two thumps on the noggin from the Master of the Revels. 'Mend this, alter this, cut this at thy peril' — and we could not do *Sir Thomas More* at all, and *Richard II* only once, and that in private. So I have been considering, Dick, and do indeed believe that one more blow at *Hamlet* might—"

"I am a player! My blood! My bones, heart and soul, all of me! In it, of it, born in a player's trunk! I know these things! I feel 'em here!" cried Dick, pulling open his doublet and thumping his chest. "But you, you, with your fine house in the country, your ox, your ass, your peaceful life among the pretty flowers, you have lost touch, Willy, you have forgot what the people want."

"Now I remember. A new play about a Jew."

"Fire-balls and squibs! Three plays straight about a Jew! The women would hate me. It's been done and done and done!"

Shakespeare spoke as gently as usual, both hands on Dick's shoulders, smiling amiably. "I thought it would be perfect for Tom Pope. A greedy, creeping, blood-lusting moneylender who hates Christians, and —"

"Tom Pope! He's old! He's bald! He's tired! Willy, I am a player. I know these things. They're bone of my bone, and I must instruct you sometimes, we all know that — now, look in my eyes, Willy, tell me, an acrobat, a clown?"

Shakespeare looked in his eyes. "A sad Jew, persecuted by triumphant Christians, like poor Dr. Lopez —"

"Persecuted by Christians! A sad Jew!"

Shakespeare went on looking in his eyes. "There's nothing on this earth, Dick, sadder than a clown."

"In life, yes! In life, yes! Yes! But on the stage! The stage!"

"Who is the very sun of light amid all the little stars at court? Who is the man whose favour will take us with him the higher he climbs? Tell me softly. In my ear, here. Whisper."

"Any fool knows it is Essex. And Essex is the general of the Queen's best troops, Essex is the darling lord of England's hopes, and Essex wants a play of war, war, war. I'll take you to him at Dover. He'll tell you so himself."

"He has a long way to go yet. I thought I would instruct him in these matters he is weak in. He hounded Lopez to his death because the foolish doctor gossiped, and disclosed that he had the French sickness. Let us show him how ugly is this intolerance of Christians toward this butt, this mendicant, this clown, this bag of rags in the gutter that creeps, and crawls, and rises to defy him to do his worst! And then, Richard, Richard, in my newly whittled *Hamlet,* I have much to learn this high and mighty he about how weakening is too much philosophy, too much French reasoning and temporizing and quibbling until a man is too windy, too bloated, too wadded up with words, words, words —"

"Yaaa!" screamed Dick. "Yaa, yaa, yow, wow, woo, wooo!"

"You are right," Shakespeare said, suddenly convinced. "It is war. Where is my tent? Where is my closet? I will start at once. Your eloquence has won me, all of me, heart, bones, blood and oons. Quick! Lead me to my parlour, my mansion-house, where it is that I sweat words."

"There, see, see, see, what man thou hast for a father, see, see, Hamnet, see? He laughs at me. At me! Me, me!"

The boy, charmed to excruciation by all this roaring attention, gazed at the great Richard Burbage with such worship in his eyes that the noisy player was struck with sudden pity.

"Damn my tripes and bones, the boy is quite worn out! We'll put him to bed at once. We've got a sick boy already in the camp."

"Oh, is it Robin?" asked Shakespeare, ready to fall from weariness himself.

"Sammy, this time. Nothing the barber surgeon could do that was not done."

They were just starting off together when the loud braying of trumpets came piercingly through the air.

"I want to see! I want to hear!" cried Hamnet, wildly excited and running to the mullioned window of the Bell. The white sails towered over the town, and there were blue, red, white, and orange pinnaces flying from the topgallant yards.

"See, Willy? I told you, people love war. Ask the boy what to write, he'll tell you."

"Can we go, father? Before they sail away?"

"They must wait for a favouring wind," Shakespeare explained. "And it's at Dover we'll see the great ships of the Fleet. These are merchantmen, adventurers, pirates, and transports for the troops."

"I'm not tired, I'm ready to go now," Hamnet said.

chapter twenty

〰〰 AND for two wild and windy months, that was how it was. From seaport town to seaport town, from North Downs to South Downs, from Battle Ridge to Selsey Bill, all the way around the Vale of Sussex to the Vale of Dorset and still westward, westward, the plodding players went, picking up soldiers' pennies, sometimes having a good afternoon in some innyard or training camp, other times not so good, and occasionally quite bad. No matter how they grumbled, and in spite of Shakespeare's painful battles with the fire-eyed maid of smoky war, as he called her in one big and bloody scene, there was one bright-eyed, eager member of the company who was always ready, who was always there, waiting with his pack and satchel to lead them on to the next camp, the next inn, the next seaport town.

"Slow, Hamnet, we must go more wisely, and more slow," his father would call to the excited, rosy-cheeked boy, with his eyes sparkling at the wonderful things he would find around the next corner.

"I'm not tired, father."

And when they were called on board a troopship or a merchantmen, and once a lovely, menacing man-of-war, it was Hamnet who made friends immediately with the highest head-man he saw, and was swarming up the shrouds and tackle to the very top of the yards. Shakespeare would gaze anxiously up, hearing a cry of triumph, and there his boy would be, hanging upside down from mizzen-skysail yard and wildly waving his Indian bonnet, given to him by a pirate.

Once they went on board the great *Ark Royal* itself, the Lord Admiral's flagship, riding at anchor off Plymouth Sound, and Hamnet sat beside old Lord Howard at supper, proud and patient as a prince, and speaking equally to all lords that spoke to him.

"A fine boy there, Mr. Shakespeare. Never saw a finer. What will you be when you grow up, Hamnet?"

"An admiral," said Hamnet, meaning it intensely. Until that gaudy day he went out with that fearsome switter-swatter, the haughty, bragging Ralegh, just back from slaughter and plunder in the golden and bounteous islands of Guiana, rings in his ears, jewels on his shoes, pouring out stories of blood and glory in steaming jungles full of naked savages, and quarrelling with everybody who dared to crowd him one little bit. Hamnet got on perfectly with this vainglorious and greedy dreamer, and was going to be everything sweet Sir Walter was, and told everybody so.

Until he met Essex, the brightest blazing star of all. That was the best day of his whole life, he whispered to his father, when they finally went to bed a little before the trumpets of sunrise woke them.

For Essex, the players rehearsed, set, lighted and staged the new play of *King John*, all about war and riot and sedition and cruel and heartless torture. And with reckless speed, Dick Burbage, Tom Pope, and Austin Philips alternately trained that boy, in secret, for a surprise to his father, in the wonderful tragic part of Prince Arthur. There in the golden daylight, on the main deck of the *Due Repulse*, with lords and officers for audience, and lamps behind bottles of coloured water to imitate night, with the salty sea wind blowing sweetly in their faces and waving their plumes and banners, the men and boys of the company spoke lines of thunder and lightning, treason and stratagems, rash, inconsiderate and fiery humours, much blood, great rioting, and churlish strife; full of flags, bullets, drums, hacked swords, and roaring war; besmeared and over-stained with slaughter's pencil, as Shakespeare regretfully said, but with some wit and beauty too, he hoped, and a wonderful tempest which swallowed up a whole armado in one afternoon.

Much pity, too, and gentleness, over the death of Prince Arthur. When Rogin Gough, in his voice as mellow as a viol, spoke the sad lines of Queen Constance, even the haughty Ralegh was seen to weep.

> "Grief fills the room up of my absent child,
> Lies in his bed, walks up and down with me,
> Puts on his pretty looks, repeats his words,
> Remembers me of all his gracious parts,
> Stuffs out his vacant garments with his form:
> Then have I reason to be fond of grief . . ."

And when young Hamnet begged his cruel jailor not with hot irons to burn out both his eyes, it was too much for old stuttering Tom Pope, and he covered his face for a moment before he could continue with his lines, as Hubert de Burgh, the rough and stubborn jailor.

And when the boy fell to his little kingdom of a forced grave, with one last cry of despair falling from the cross-jack yard, an awful knowledge, cold as the last death of all love in the world, struck his father to the heart.

They have tricked me, and turned my own best hope against me.

He ran to the net the players had rigged to catch the boy, the rage beating in his brain. Hamnet was laughing and unbroken, behind the wall of sticks and canvas.

"Was it what you wanted, father?"

But Shakespeare turned from him to these painted players with their goggle eyes, false hair and tinsel, and muttered between his teeth, "Fools, who have trapped my gentle falcon in your net! Was this your sport, to use my words, my weakness, and my shame against me? This is no glory, to be the sport of fools!"

Then the trumpets summoned them for the last braying and bragging scene, and then would come the jig, when if the painted players had pleased the lords and officers, some coins would jingle on the deck.

But now, through his jingling lines before the lords in the

ribbons, feathers, jewels and golden chains that signified their merit, the trembling father was haunted by the stricken face of his little son. Oh, I am a fool, a motley fool, a clown, to have dreamed of anything for the son of a player but muddy inn-yards, pennies from our betters, and scraps from the rich men's table. He was speaking the last lines:

> "This England never did, nor never shall
> Lie at the proud foot of a conqueror
> But when it first did help to wound itself . . ."

Lost in a blur of words, while time swelled and encompassed a whole lifetime of windy words and vanity, in the small person of a poor player strutting through his little moments under the sun and into darkness, mud and rain. A fine lady's coach whirls past and in the street a booby laughs at the player's face spattered with mud.

My face is daubed red, white and black, and I'm the bastard braggart of this windy show.

Among the tinsel lace, the copper crowns and coronets of the gaudy players thronged about him, in their handed-down robes and rusty armour, he still saw the stricken face of his little son, still saw him turning away blind with tears, and all the lovely light gone out of him.

Oh God, he is my son, my own, doomed like me to walk the earth like a shadow in the sun, a very nothing tricked out in false and borrowed words.

The players were bowing low before the lords of high blood, great power and hereditary worth.

"What's with thee, Willy, for God's sake? And where's thy boy?" Old Tom Pope, tricked out in all the gilt and slashings of William Longsword, the Earl of Salisbury.

Shakespeare was now bent low before the magnanimous young Earl, muttering more words of thanks, more words of humble duty to this boy with a beard coming. The flutes and viols were striking up the jig, and as Shakespeare rose and stepped backward in deep reverence before these lordships he saw whirling in the bloody sunset light the copper crowns and tinsel of his fellow players, dancing for pennies, and if the good lords still liked them enough at supper-time, perhaps some bread and wine and leftover meats too, at the common table for them among the sailors.

Tom Pope and Austin Philips saw their distracted word-man hurrying about the deck and heard him calling the name of his son. And many seamen saw him and heard him that night, hunting all over the ship, or in the quarters where common players might be allowed.

chapter twenty-one

❦❦ *WHAT I wanted will be never. The dream of an idiot splashing in the gutters of a hundred towns in the country of fools.*

From Plymouth he did not know where to go. The players were still picking up pennies in alehouse yards and in the camps, waiting until the great ships sailed against the Spaniards. But when? When? Young Essex was grappling with the giddy Queen, all hope one day, all despair the next, ordered and counter-ordered, blandishments his meed one day, and bitter reproaches and humiliations the next.

He had no time for any encouragement for such men of shadows as the players.

Not on any of the armed ships or the merchantmen. Not in the darkest corner of any scullery or almshouse.

"I fear that Willy's no good for us until he finds the boy," Dick Burbage muttered to Jack Heminge, the most trusted man in the company.

"He'll fall into a sickness," Heminge said.

"He's done it before. I've seen him that crazed with black melancholy not even his holy woman dared bless him. Even poor ailing Mrs. Lynn warned me not to cross him."

"He should have praised the boy," Burbage said.

"I think he wants him to be a gentleman, not trash like us. Clowns, strutting crows trying to be peacocks. A pity he has not got his house in the country, his poor small trick of arms, so that he could be another fatheaded squire, fitted to stand four paces behind some country lordship, and pay his levies of horse and armour to the Queen's high constables. Oh God, I could laugh at him, if I did not need to weep."

"The boy was good, even though Willy spoke not a word to him, and hid away after. What is it in the man that makes

140

him turn all wild and bitter, after whole weeks of sunny good
nature and such patience he could bend even the royal shrew
of all shrews to his gentle will?"

Tom Pope speaking.

"Hush," said Heminge. "We're only players, remember. Not
even grooms, or fit to hold the basin for a lordship to puke in."

"What Willy does about the boy is not our business," said
Henry Cundall. "My own boys will go into the fish business
and make good money, and my girl will marry a member of
the pewterers' company, and hold up her head on any street.
Would that Ben Jonson had not made the boy lust after glory
as a player. It is a little wee glory, that is blown out in an
afternoon. Will is right to want something better for the boy
than what is in store for us."

"But damn my bones and briskets, why does not Willy
speak his bitterness or his anger like any man of plain old
tripes and guts? Like me, when I beat my boys and hold them
to the line laid down for 'em?"

"I've heard him called gentle by this one and that one,"
said Burbage with a hopeless sigh, "who were full of love and
admiration for the man of all those pretty words and proper
sentiments. But those who speak thus have not seen him as I
have, torn by a rage so great that it would seem to make his
eyes start from his head, while he tore his hair and raked his
flesh with his nails, and still not speaking a word. That was
when I learnt better than to be gentle, soft, and mannerly like
my poor mad friend, who cannot speak his madness, for fear
it would crack him, or burn him to a cinder. He could not
tell the boy. How could he tell the boy? He has all hell in him
at times like that. But I wish he would not hide himself away
from us."

"Kit Marlowe spewed it out in drink," said Heminge.

"Ay, and Greene too, and Tom Kyd, and Peele, all of 'em in
the old days, they were tosspots."

"And all died in the gutter," Henry Cundall said, rising
and stalking away from them.

Time for the players to pick up their sticks and stocks, pack their trunks and baskets, load up their gaudy, jolting cart, beat the poor jades' saddles to put a few more flocks in the thin places that rubbed their sores, and when all was loaded in, and they had paid their score at the flea-bitten inn that gave them a corner or two, then they must go trudging off up the Vale of Exe, many and many a weary mile among the moors and across the filthy barren ground near Severn Sea, until at last they came to Bristol, beyond the chilling ranges of the black Welsh mountains, and were nearly in sight of the friendly Cotswolds.

Not much muttered about wars and glory here, and less than that among the players. The great expedition to lift the siege of Calais had fizzled out like a wet squib between one pompous speech and another by one general or another. Unlucky lords and soldiers, marching and countermarching back and forth for months and months, prepared to slaughter, plunder, kill, burn, and pull down every Spanish fortification from Grey-nose Cape to Pig-fat Creek in the Country of the Frog-king. The maddening Queen, promising help to King Henri and repenting before the news had even reached the baffled Frenchman, dangling her favour and withdrawing it sixteen times in a week from the steaming, stamping Essex, had finally driven the desperate Earl to sail off for a last hopeless foray against the very heart of the Spanish treasure fleet at Cadiz, to risk all and gain all, to fling all away on one wild storm at sea, or wrest bright honour from the pale-faced moon, as Shakespeare would say if he were there.

"Those damned Frogs never would keep any engagement," said a sheepherder at Penstoke, shaking his head over all the starving, broken seamen bedevilling the port country, from Drake and Hawkins's last expedition to the West Indies.

"Not their fault they had to give in to the Spaniards," Dick Burbage muttered, under his breath. "By God, they waited months for the Queen to keep her word. But which word? I would not be Essex for all the rubies in the Escorial. He waited and waited too, until half his troops and the best of his stores were gone, stolen and gnawed away."

But old Heminge hushed him before he would say any more, and rouse the petty constables against lewd players who were not much wanted anyway. Riots in the market towns, because of the continued dearth, snatching and catching among the unruly people; many beggars now and some with forged licenses.

"The poor are up," the host at that rude inn said. "Lord, Lord, I think our lords are in the wrong war, at the wrong time, and in the wrong place for poor hungry England."

Even the gipsies were starving now. It was told by a sutler at this inn that old Topcliffe himself, recently disgraced for bragging too loudly of bribes paid the Lord Keeper Puckering, had been let out of Westminster Gaol and set loose, with his rack, upon the gipsies of Northamptonshire.

chapter twenty-two

வ⁣ஷ BUTTER riots in London, whippings and the pillory, proclamations against rebellion, and as an example to the people, five youths hanged, drawn and quartered for throwing stones at the warden of the Tower, on a Sunday afternoon in June.

While the Queen and Council did their best and worst to keep the people down, it was rumoured that the players and other lewd fellows plotted more riots and disorders. Clearly this was a crisis, and called for stern measures. Orders went out to the high constables of every hundred, the petty constables of every borough, the squires and gentlemen of property, the aldermen and burgesses of every town, and to all trade guilds, and to all brotherhoods, and to all courts, juries, magistrates, and justices of the peace, to put those bad men down, lock them up, or drive them out, or hurry them on, and levy fines upon them, and if any were caught attempting to incite, persuade, solicit, or commit any nuisance, mischief or inconvenience whatsoever or howsoever to disturb or hinder the ministers and parishioners in time of divine service, or any other time, they were to be suppressed, their lewd and ungodly practices were to be ended, and all such evil and disordered people were to be kept in order, and all playhouses, and all their stages, galleries and rooms were to be shut, closed, defaced and plucked down.

The plague-sores of cities, the scandal of suburbs, the excrement of earth — so the common players were termed, in pulpit and parish wherever they lurked.

And the more they were put down, the more the rebellious youth of the towns and cities arose and struck back at the worried citizens. They roughed them up in the streets; they pulled up their skirts and cloaks in the alleys; they choked and gouged and beat good and peaceful citizens for any reason, or for no reason but youth, which was wanton. Alas,

alas, it was the evil plays, full of rioting and lechery. Would no sound and upright man among the bawdy players ever come forth to celebrate right conduct, good order, pious thinking and gentle breeding?

Someone should pay for the wild disorder in the country! And two especially harmful and superfluous species of people did. First, the staring blackamoors, all eyes and lips, who had been herded into the dock districts by the returning heroes from the late calamitous expedition to Guiana.

Out with them!

Second, the stubborn players who yet clung to their low and immoral bowsing-houses and vulgar inns, hoping for better times and a harvest of pennies.

Away, ye men of Satan!

Some of the cargo boats carrying the blackamoors off to Portugal passed the first proud ships coming in from the glorious triumph at Cadiz. A few raggle-taggle players stopped to cheer the officers and feathered lordships parading up Cheapside, with torches, pipes and drums. The quarrels over the booty taken from the Spanish ships that had not burned in Cadiz Harbour had not yet begun.

This glory Shakespeare did not see. One day in the Blackfriars Gatehouse, whispering with Mrs. Lynn in a secret room where she now sheltered Father Gerard and other missionary priests hiding from the executioners, he heard the word he had been hoping for these many bitter weeks.

"One night in the darkness I heard an owl hooting in the garden of the Sores' house," whispered the holy woman. "It was our signal that I myself taught the boy when he was hiding with us."

Shakespeare trembled as the leaves of time rustled and blurred before his smarting eyes. Where and when? In what lost childhood?

In the orchard of my father's house, I heard Dick Field hooting like a staring owl, and climbed down the ragged apple-tree.

"Did he come in?" he asked her, sick with fear.

"No, he dared not show his poor face. Blessed Mother Mary, how wasted the child was when I crept out to him there in the foggy night and made him come in! Mrs. Dolly cried in the soup she placed before him."

"And where did he go then?"

"Jesus and Mary forgive me for not taking the child with me when I fled from Topcliffe and Justice Gardiner that very night! He told me something, I did not catch the words too well, he was so wild to go. But I remember the name of that poor distracted man you were so kind to."

"God bless you for that. But what man was that?"

"Why, that poor ragged hungry man in his old coachman's cloak, quoting Greek out of one side of his mouth and Latin the other, and so disputatiously striving to reform me of my religion that I never got the chance to tell him more than good morrow, and he would dispute me that."

Shakespeare was shaking with a chill now, or with haste to be gone.

"I should have known," he said, pressing her frail hand, worn and roughened by toil, though it was the hand of a highborn lady. "The man who taught him to be a player, and would have taught me how to write plays too, if he'd had the time. Oh, my prophetic soul! Ben Jonson."

"Stay and rest your weary heart and mind," Mrs. Lynn implored him. "You are as pale and wan as the boy."

"Thanks, but I'm not tired," he said. "I'll find Ben in Westminster, or Holborn, or in the Swan perhaps."

"Dear soul, they closed the Swan, and all your playhouses, and will pull them all down," she warned him, at the secret passageway which led down to the river-stairs.

"Good night, sweet friend, and God have mercy on my boy. Remember him in your orisons. Good night."

So he was gone, and he never saw her again this side of the bloody scaffold, where she was carried one dark day and hanged for harbouring a seminary priest. It was said that her limbs were so wasted by sickness that they were no bigger than the rope around her neck. One witness in the crowd said that so far from repenting, she cried at the last, "I wish, with all my soul, that where I had entertained one, I could have entertained a thousand."

chapter twenty-three

ꝦꝦ "GOG'S wounds, who am I, a poor disarted woman, to know that man's comings and goings?"

So the rough, square-edged goodwife of the missing cat-man, when the tired hunter found her in her corner behind the scullery, nursing her new baby, a boy with red hair, named Benjamin.

Here at the Black Bell in Carter Lane, where all the rough brutal grooms and carters fought and patched up their quarrels in order to fight again, a child was born, a son was given to the missing scholar.

The baby seemed to be a good baby, not strong, but his eyes and ears looked promising, and his tiny fingers curled like sea-fronds over a mermaid's breast.

Shakespeare scribbled down his name and his message, ever the one and ever the same, wished the complaining woman good cheer and an early return of that man she called the walking woe of her hard life, and departed for some other scene of the cat-man's obscure and creeping journey through the thick, dark ignorance of a world that knew him not.

Where now? Into the provinces again, to find him with some scurvy company of jugglers and acrobats, a master of motions at a Punch and Judy show?

When he was but a raw and lubberly boy and I was scratching love-poems in my corner at Dick Field's printing shop, I swear it was Ben I caught putting on a monstrous parody of my very poems on the youth with curls of the hue of marjoram blossoms, and the filthy slut who stole him from me. What did he call it, now? *Hero and Leander? Friendship's True Trial?* A wicked wit he had then, before it was all snowed under with scholarship.

I wonder how many innocent wenches with dark eyes and

148

how many pretty youths of birth and breeding the silly people say I loved and lost to make a sheaf of poems. Pray heaven nobody will ever know the true theme of my art in those days, which was the begetting of money upon the body of that strumpet, Fortune. The only wench I lay with in my hungry apprenticeship, and she but gave me a burning.

Well, poor Willy Honyng is gone now from the Master of the Revels' favour and preferment, and has married himself to a country daughter of fat flocks and herds, barns and manure piles, at Bury St. Edmund's, I've heard. Resigned in some disgrace for withholding the wages of the poor carpenters and quarrelling with poor old doting Edmund Tilney. If he were but here now I might find some little favour myself, for a brace of new sonnets to someone's eyebrows and nostrils, or whatever is the rage now among the fancy.

At least I used old Edmund's lamentatious exhortations for the dear young squib to heat up some good woman's bed.

Not so young either . . . though he looked a beardless boy, I think Willy the Honey was some thirty years and well past the ambush of young days. Some of these Suffolk people keep the damask of their county's roses in their cheeks, well after the coarser kind, like me, are beated and chopped, as I called it somewhere, with tanned antiquity.

And my unkind patron got the twenty marrying sonnets next. And a fat price from loving Mary, his mother, if I had only used it for some house, any house. Before the fire burned half of Stratford, or a good third anyway. And the wind came to blow through the ruins of my hopes and plans.

My boy in some cold corner, hiding from my wrath, when only to see that light flame up in him and hear his lovely speech again I would give him all the honey of my fancy for a new play to dance and sing and charm the lordships with again.

Heaven forgive me too. My boy would, on the instant, if we could look at each other again.

Wandering the muddy alleys of the quarters known to have

been favoured by Ben Jonson, the ancient song, oldest of any sung by the English race, wailing in his mind:

Westron wynd, when will thou blow?
The small rain down doth rain.
O if my love were in my arms,
And I in my bed again!

He sang it to me, that night at old Jack Sore's, when we were merry. And poor Doll wept at it, and we all had to console her, and kiss her over and over.

How many mothers has the boy had? In place of that one who wanders in the sick country of grief, only hearing her own lamentations?

Sweet Doll, and Mrs. Lynn, and Davenant's wife at the Crown, and my tight patron's loose mother . . .

Lady Jocosa whispered that afternoon it rained and we were caught under the great mulberry bush in the park, "Oh, Willy darling, if only you'd found me that night at Gray's Inn, when I ran from you after I kissed you, and I waited and waited and waited, burning, burning, and you never came . . ."

Youth never knows, but if it only did . . .

"Sweet jack-in-the-bushes, if you'd but found me, instead of these tiresome children with their big noses and horse-teeth, we might have had such a lovely monster together!"

That was why she asked me to bring Hamnet once, there in the garden of Clopton House, and Anne was angry at me, but I took him, and she kissed and petted him, and said he was so like somebody she could have loved to death, if things about life had not made it impossible.

Not think of hot wenches and cold wives any more. Find Jonson. Seek out the cat-man.

Among the fripparias on Cornhill, the sellers of old apparel and household stuff, among the clattering of pewter pots and the voices of cooks crying hot ribs of beef roasted, and pies

well baked, he met a poulterer's man who told him that Topcliffe had that pockmarked, red-headed puppet-master in his
house along Bridewell. "He'll not curse again on Sunday, master," said the poulterer's man, busy scalding and dressing
chicken carcasses over a charcoal fire.

"I thought Mr. Topcliffe was no longer in London."

"Try the Gatehouse, master. And listen well in the deep and
dark of night."

And now St. Jude, patron of lost causes, be with me, and
with the thieves, whores, Jews, blackamoors and all unwanted
and superfluous men. Oh, I could write a play for angels to
weep at, and the godly to hiss out of every parish. I would
bed a pure virgin with a lusty Moor, I would daub blood on
the moon's pocky face as witness to all evil, I would trap
Beelzebub behind the high altar, and melt glacial virtue in a
pious maid with the burning coal of pity in a squalid groom.
Rise, sin! Fall, virtue! And let no eye of justice spy me out in
my creeping.

In less than an hour, in the Cockle room at the Mermaid,
in Bread Street, he was huddled over a table in a dark corner
with Tom Savage, goldsmith, vintner, and measurer of sea
coals to the city of London, likewise landlord to old Jack
Heminge, and neighbour to Mountjoy the tire maker in Silver
Street.

"I think we could," said this solid and versatile citizen.

"A coal barge?"

"With a secret hatch for wine."

"Will your man be waiting?"

"Below the Gatehouse, at Puddle Dock."

"The godly keepers share a common taste for sweet wines
with the old friars?"

"There are gates provided for all kinds, my boy. Why, that
hill, nigh the dock, down away under, is a maze of tunnels
and secret caves, and was still in holy King Edward's time.
Oh, there's more known of your great palaces and your prisons

too, by such vintners and sea coal men as are of the ancient company, than these fools here now above ground would even dream goes on deep down below 'em; but the rats know all."

"I'm the rats' man then. Where shall we meet again?"

"Be at the tire maker's house, any Wednesday, and hang a lantern at Muggle Street corner."

"I'll hang it, or be hanged."

chapter twenty-four

CREEPING up the bankside and into the ditch along
Bride Lane, he reached down in the pitchy dark and touched
the slimy mouth of the conduit.

Open.

May all the devils of this accursed place be thanked for
their ignorance of this hell-mouth.

So by the same dark and narrow way he had come from
his last visit with Mrs. Lynn, he now passed beneath the
ancient house of the Hanging Sword and was in the secret
tunnel to the Gatehouse of Blackfriars.

God of mercy, if the prince of tortures has not got Mrs.
Lynn, I will believe for life. He must have pounced upon her
the very day I was here. In darkness of night, a jackal skulking
upon his sleeping prey.

A steady dripping of water upon these stones. The ditch
turns here.

And now beyond this grating, the fetid breath of Bridewell.

Now he heard some prisoner of darkness groaning on the
stones, and cursing in Latin.

Is it good Latin? Or is it bad Latin?

> *"Fuit, fuit, fuit, haec sapientia quondam,*
> *Publica privatis secernere, sacra profanis,*
> *Concubitu prohibere vago . . ."*

Great gods and nymphs of the heavenly fields, it is the
loveliest Latin that ever I heard in an accursed cave.

The cat-man not only lives, breathes, groans, curses, but he
maintains a nice discrimination between things sacred and
profane. And when he quotes, he quotes from Horace.

Raising both hands to the sill of the grating, he pulled himself up and crouched there while feeling for the secret latch.

153

"*Quod hoc sibi vult?*" came the hoarse voice of the prisoner. Meaning, what do you want here?

"*Libraminem,*" answered Shakespeare, nearly falling. That is to say, I'd like to keep my balance.

"Who art thou? I fear thee not," snarled Ben.

"Shakescene the Shaky," replied the insecure but persistent poet, wearing his knuckles raw on the rusty hasp.

"Oh God, my prayers have been answered! Or have they got thee too?"

"Not yet, little cat-man. And now silence."

Crash! A pair of pliers fell.

He could hear Ben muttering curses in Greek.

Awful stirrings and rustlings over these slimy stones. Little wet feet ran over Shakespeare's face.

"Now, my boy, if you can stand."

"Better than ever," said Ben, and now Shakespeare thought he could discern, like a live coal in a heap of ashes, the cat-man's boring eye.

"No chains? Manacles?"

"I wrote a love song for the keeper to sing to Black Lucy of Clerkenwell, and he struck 'em off."

"Reach up and clasp my wrists."

"Sweet wight of Warwickshire, I'll never criticize thy verses again."

"Hold hard. Now up, up, and in through here."

Some hard grunting, scratching, scraping, and scrambling, and Ben was through the grating and down on the slippery stones beside him.

"By heaven, I'll repent my sins and be good from now on," said the cat-man. "I'll go home, kiss my wife —"

"Softly now, like Tib in the house of rats," whispered Shakespeare. "And promise not too much yet. Save a little until we are safe."

An unknown time later they were lying in the belly of a coal-heaver's barge and bearing in to St. Saviour's Stairs.

"Where, Willy?"

"Doll Sore's house on Bankside."

"Oh no, I cannot go. It was there the justice's man found me out and made hell's own uproar for Doll and Jack."

"But he found no priest? Or Mrs. Lynn?"

"I know not where she lies, but Topcliffe has her house now. And has Father Gerard spread-eagled and chained to a wall."

"I fear for them, Ben. And for my boy."

Ben told him then what he needed to know.

"The boy is safe and sound. I put him in the care of a pack-horse carrier who would take him home to his mother."

"Oh God, I'll repent too, and lead a harmless life."

"Will, the boy was strange. Wore the rude dress of a ship's boy, and would not talk of playing."

"That was the last dress he wore in *King John*. Did he tell where he has been since our night on the deck of the *Due Repulse?*"

"Not much, my friend. He seemed sore distraught. Only wanted to prove himself better than a cause of grief to his father."

"Cause of grief!"

"I think there was something in his heart that would not be appeased. Though he would not weep, nor speak any word of blame."

"Oh, Ben, if I could have told him what was in my heart! He must have been wet, cold, hungry, alone, and fearful all these weeks —"

"Oh, no, Willy, the last thing he said was, as he kissed me farewell and he mounted this carrier's pack horse: *Be easy, Ben, I'm not afraid.*"

Shakespeare could not speak, only clasped his hand.

"There was never so gentle a son of a gentle father," said Ben, as they crawled out of the hold and prepared to climb up St. Saviour's Stairs. "In my darkest night I still see a star. Remember me to him, Willy, and be kind."

That was when Shakespeare remembered to inform Ben that he too was a father, and had a fair new son.

"He is as like thee as an egg," said Shakespeare.

"I'll name him William, after the Conqueror of Locks and Dungeons."

"Too late! She's named him Ben."

Now the cat-man was mute, and they embraced, and were parting, when Ben remembered the name of the carrier.

"It was some species of gravel. Grevil . . . Grenfell . . . Greville . . . Greenfield . . ."

"Greenway, Willy Greenway! A little, squinch-eyed man, with a blue tooth?"

"That's he! Said he knew the in and out of thy whole country, and would cherish the boy like one of his own thirteen."

"Oh, wonderful! I'll ride to Stratford as soon as I've washed this filthy witness from my body, and borrowed a shirt and hose from Jack."

"And I'll to my wife, and my new son! And never show my face where Topcliffe or any jackal of justice can find me out."

With all blinds closed, and not a light showing through any chink, Jack Sore and his wife made the wet and muddy man warm and merry.

"Fear no more, old friend. It is over a fortnight the boy has been gone. Any day now you will have a letter from home, saying he is safe and well."

But yet Shakespeare could not sleep that night, and the dawn leaking in over his window sill found him on his knees. When he heard old Jack stirring he lay down again, and it was then that sleep came down heavily upon him.

Doll Sore was on the stairs, whispering.

Why was she waiting? Was she listening to hear if he wept in his dreams? And why would he be weeping?

He looked up at the grey windowpanes, and saw the misty brick and half-timbered wall of the tailor's shop across the lane. Love Lane. And why would he be laughing?

His dusty heaps of old tattered plays and sixpenny books got in his way as he leaped up, and he knocked them down. No more, no more picking up scraps from Fortune's table.

A new life now, a life for the boy. And Anne too, if only she could come back to meet him over the wastes of the years.

He hurried to the door.

Doll stood in the hallway, trembling all over. As he looked at her she burst into tears and flung her apron over her face.

"What now, sweet Doll? Has Jack been at his carwhitchets again?"

A loud sob from under the apron, and then lifting it just enough to see her way down the stairs, she fled.

A cold shivering seized him. It was August, yet he felt the chill of death.

He heard old Jack now down there, swearing and sighing. Then he started up the stairs like a sergeant making an arrest.

"What is it, Jack? What's the matter?" His lips were stiff with fear.

The fat and sweating host, with big tears on his cheeks, held out a paper in his trembling hand.

Shakespeare muttered impatiently that people must not send to him any more in London. He was a man marked for justice here. All players must be gone from London.

"The carrier. He brought it, and asked me to give it to you if I knew where you lay."

Shakespeare took the paper, broke the seal, unfolded it.

The words written on this letter paper were as strange as any dream. He kept reading them as if he had never learned to join meaning to words.

One single word at the top, in the rare painful hand of Anne, learned at much trouble to please him.

Come

And then the careful penmanship of his mother, who had been trained in the School of Dames:

My deare beloued Son:
It is wyth a sore & distressed hart that I must tell thee bitter newes. My onlie grandson & thy son Hamlett fell sick of a bad

feever shortlie after hee returned to us all weake & worne on the Feast of Stephen. Thy father never slept a nighte but watched by hys bed. Thy wyfe arose from her owne sick-bed and dyd come to nurse hym. In three dayes hee died. Alas poore chyld wee knowe not what was in his trobled hart. Maye our Blesed Lord & Hys aungels receeve him to eternall reste. Come home deare Son to thy wyfe, shee is sore distraught.

> *Mary thy Mother, thys xi august Feaste*
> *of St. Susanna.*

It was thoughte wise bye the Council & Mr. Quyney thatte he sholde be bured this same daie for feare of pestilence.

He stood there muttering stupidly, not knowing that the blow had been struck.

"I must look at this paper with more light. Please to enter, Jack. There's wine from France."

He shivered again, and took the paper to the window.

Now he looked up, stammered something to Jack, looked all round the room, and saw darkness, and whirling light.

Still he did not know, and smiled at Jack as the man put both hands on his shoulders and looked into his eyes. "The carrier told us, Will. Old Greenway from Stratford brought the letter and told us."

"Told you?"

"Hear me, Will. Your little son is dead and buried. A good funeral, a very good funeral. Many people went, he said. Listen to me now. You have overtired yourself, you have worked too late, too many nights . . ."

But he shook him off, went to the table and poured two cups of the good wine from Burgundy, smuggled in by his own patron, kind and generous again now. An arrangement with the Danvers brothers, he was vaguely explaining to Jack, and with Lord Ashley, from the plunder taken at Cadiz.

Then as in a waking dream, as if the boy were still playing and laughing downstairs, he was sure he heard Hamnet rehearsing with Ben Jonson in the Dolphin Room, as they had done so often.

"He's calling me, he wants me, Jack."

That was when Jack took him gently in his arms and shook him, as if out of sleep.

"Hear me, Will, dear friend. Hear me now. Hamnet is dead and buried, in your town of Stratford."

"I hear him, he wants me," Shakespeare said, pulled away from Jack and hurried downstairs and into the Dolphin Room. Two commercial travellers deep in confabulation looked up angrily at his unmannerly interruption, and the old one said, "Prithee, good sir, let us be private here!"

Shakespeare hastily muttered an apology and retreated to the front parlour, where a happy family of provincial travellers sat at supper: father, mother, elder son, little son and a pretty laughing daughter. No one else in the room.

"Good Will, come in with us, let us have supper together," said Doll Sore, putting her trembling hand on his arm.

"Thank you, Doll, but I am not hungry. I have a long way to go," he answered, and suddenly the whole meaning of the words blazed into his brain, and he knew all that had happened, all of it.

"It's the way of us all, we must all go in the end," she was saying. He nodded and smiled, pressed her hand, and went quickly up the stairs and into his room in a strange house, in a strange country. After he closed the door very gently he fell to his knees, as if struck down. He remained there, with no tears, while through his mind went swarming images of a green misty country, cloudy and sunny beneath the sky of childhood, and he heard the roaring of water in the eddy by Clopton Bridge. And the laughter of a young brave voice, all about him the happy laughter, in the sweet air, in the singing trees, in time's ceaseless stream.

"My boy, my boy, my boy," he said, and wept at last.

Book Three

S W A N

O F

A V O N

Sweet Swan of Avon! *what a sight it were*
To see thee in our waters yet appeare,
And make those flights upon the bankes of Thames,
That so did take Eliza, *and our* James!

Ben Jonson:
To the memory of my beloved,
The AUTHOR
Mr. WILLIAM SHAKESPEARE:
AND
what he hath left us.

chapter twenty-five

NOTHING would please the Queen that morning.

"Alas, her Majesty is sore distempered," whispered poor Robert Cecil, her new Principal Secretary, as not one, but two maids of honour ran weeping from the shrieking, stamping, swearing Queen, their cheeks slapped, their ears boxed. Merely for tiptoeing through the Privy Galleries to peep out at the handsome Earl of Essex, with his great new beard, playing football with Southampton, Mountjoy, Ashley and Harington.

"This boy, this upstart boy who has risen so high by my will and by his wits, by God I'll put him down too!" shouted the furious Queen. "Fifty thousand pounds for his burning and pillaging at Cadiz, and what have I got for it? Trouble, famine, riot, uprisings among my people, and the savage Irish revolting again! He's driving me distracted with his triumphs, and all his little new knights! By God I'll put them down too!"

She raved about the bearded boy, she raved about the

163

Council, about old Burleigh and his hunchbacked son, about Lady Rich and Lady Russell and Lady Bridges, and all her untrustworthy ladies who simply refused to remain virgins even though she had so ordered them.

Poor little hunchbacked Robert Cecil's narrow knees were getting so stiff with all this kneeling and listening that any moment now he would have to move somehow, up, down or sideways. He spoke up finally and tried to point out to the raving lady that young Essex has been a good general in Cadiz and done much honour to the realm in burning and sacking the Spanish ships; but this was fatally wrong, and made her so mad she drove him and three others straightway from the presence, with orders to remain away from her by ten miles.

Anthony Ashley, who had brought her the news of the triumph at Cadiz, she drove forth for dealing in plunder and pillage with the Earl of Southampton. The pretty Southampton, who had sulked and simpered about her all the while that Essex had been triumphing, she cursed for having no beard or no wife yet, and furnishing her no free entertainment as any worshipping lord should have done, who had a brain or a heart. And John Harington, her handsome long-legged godson, she told to get away from her and stay away from her and not come near her again. Writing a vulgar pamphlet upon his revolutionary invention, a water-closet! Shocking! Away with 'em all! Handsome, young, scornful, self-ish, selfish, selfish popinjay lords she had made herself and would unmake again, by God! Pretty prating maids of honour without honour, always sneaking and peeking and lusting after her devoted gentlemen who were not gentlemen but robbers, robbers, robbers, and driving their poor old Queen and her poor old kingdom to ruin, ruin, ruin!

The best thing pretty Hal of Southampton could think of was to put on a damned expensive pageant for the miserly old woman.

"It's sure to fetch her," said Essex, plunging out of his tub and dripping all over the costly parquet floor as his two body-servants pursued him with French towels, and his barber prepared honey water and gold dust for his flourishing beard.

"A tiltyard entertainment at Tichfield, perhaps?" said Hal.

"Been done better at Whitehall and Hampton Court. Mustn't push too hard, my boy," Essex said.

"M-no, and then too, they're so rough," said Hal. "Cheaper just to lend my badge to a company of players, and let their writing fellows cobble me up something immensely flattering for the old woman."

"Whatever happened to your man Shakespeare?" Essex asked, now being towelled by his men. "Man vanished right off my ship and never came to thank me for letting his fellows play a thing about King John for me."

Southampton knocked sharply on his skull with his fan. "Bless my briskets! I wonder where my Willy has been all summer!"

"A good fellow at the game. I'd steal him myself, if I could afford a company."

"What would she like, Robert? I swear the man can write anything. A masking show, say in Venice?"

Essex shrugged his way out of the French towels and accepted a pair of respectfully offered underdrawers from his favourite groom. "Oh, I'm tired of all that Italian stuff. It's stale. Give her a good, stiff, cynical, mocking comedy in the latest French manner. Full of despair and doubt, you know — civilized. She'll love that."

"It sounds perfect, Hal!" cried Southampton eagerly, coming face to face with his own personal spy again, the ever-following Florio.

"What is perfect, my sweet master?" simpered the sly Italian.

"Not you," said Hal, backing up and treading on the dragging tail of Bungay, the pet lime-hound of Boy Jack Harington, the Queen's pet godson.

In the yapping confusion he was able to escape from the sneaking spy into the Queen's own privy garden, where none but her very upmost men were ever permitted.

"Great socks, Hal, what seek you here?" muttered Boy Jack himself, who was supervising the erection of a peculiar Turkish, or possibly Persian, kiosk in a bower of clipped lavender and dwarf box.

"Ah, Jack, you're a poet. In your rambles, have you seen my Willy anywhere? It is crucial, it is indeed."

"By Apollo, man, this is no place to be at this moment. What Willy, for God's sake?"

"My Willy, my Willy the Shakespeare, my poet, my playwright. He must be yet living, but where?"

Arching his fine slender neck, he stared all around the privy garden, as if expecting his Willy to materialize from behind a shrub.

"Oh, the fellow who wrote those sonnets to some black wench. I hear he died of a surfeit. Or was that some other scribbler?"

"Two others," said the inquisitive Earl, poking his nose inside the hauntingly familiar structure. Two baleful eyes in a pale pocky face, which was topped off with alarming red hair, glared at him like cats' eyes.

"For God's sake, Hal, come out of that! It's for her Majesty's sixty-fourth birthday," muttered Boy Jack Harington.

The startled Earl was in a state of wonderful torture: to find out more of this delicious secret, or to save himself from known and unknown dangers? His graceful figure was arrested between irresistible advance and inevitable retreat.

"But who's *in* there? Haven't I seen that face before?"

"Now, now, now, there's a good lad, why not go find Liz Vernon and see what she wants?" Harington cooed, his arms around the dithering Earl.

"What *are* you up to, Jack? Is it what I think it is?"

"Look, my dear boy, I've tried the old girl with poetry, and she spat on it. I've given her a crystal bowl, *slightly* garnished with gold, and broken. I've given her a heart of gold garnished with sparks of rubies, with a branch of red and white diamond and ruby roses. *Nothing* will please her. What was I to *do?*"

"I tried her with poetry too," said the mysterious monster from within.

"Who *is* that in there?" cried Southampton, stamping.

"A versatile and loyal subject," said Ben Jonson, stepping out of the royal kiosk, or whatever it was. "Test the plumbing now, will you, Sir Jack? The fountain, the pipes, the big brass sluice, and the brickwork are now perfection itself, and I think she'll like you for your privy if not for your poetry."

The royal godson eagerly stepped inside. An awed pause. Then a rather ominous roaring, as of a waterfall.

"Eureka!" he said, emerging all smiles.

"How exciting!" cried Hal. "Let me try it!"

"Never!" said Boy Jack, barring the way. "It is sacred."

Meanwhile Ben was calmly gathering his wrenches and trowels.

"Oh, oh, you'll be famous, Jack!" Southampton cried, clapping him on the shoulders and kissing him. "Think of it! Millions shall arise up and call thee blessed."

"They would do better to be seated," Ben said. "Now pay me, sir."

"Oh Jackie, what's it to be called?" twittered the Earl.

"The Roaring Girl?" said Harington. "No, French is more fashionable. I'll baptize it *Jacques à l'Eau,* in memory of my name and my naval training."

Ben snorted, whether over the payment Harington discreetly slipped him or the excited young men's nomenclature. "Loo it is, a fine word for necessary shelter among the Scots. Anglo-Saxon, *hleo.* With Roman sophistication. The French have no part in it at all."

"Now I know this fellow!" cried Hal. "Another inhibited player come to roost! Tibalt the cat-man, in my own Willy's play! Your death all over the stage was splendid. But where *is* my Willy"

"Making the best of this exile, as I am," growled Ben, walking right away from him toward the water-stairs.

"Oh, can you hurry and fetch him for me? And for the Queen?" cried the Earl, hurrying after him.

"Now I'll tell you, my Lord," Ben said, turning sharply round and looking him as straight in the eyes as he could with his own set in so crooked. "The man is grieved unto death. And may God forgive me as He forgives you. Blind! We've been blind!"

"No man in your station, whatever it is, has dared to speak to me so," the Earl said in amazement. "There is truth in your words that quite confounds me."

Ben nodded his rocky head in agreement to that. *"Deo adjuvante, non timendum, sed eventus stultorum magister,"** he said, rolling out those sonorous vowels with gusto.

"This is the strangest bricklayer that ever I saw," murmured the Earl.

"I merely lay my bricks or my words in order and according to right principles," said Ben. "Well, how much do you want to send to your Willy? It might cost you more than it once did."

"He lives? He breathes? He eats?" said young Hal.

"The man is in sore grief. He mourns the death of the only son he will ever have — that is, legitimate — and his wife is no help, being sick of a melancholy humour."

"He was the most feeling poet that ever wrote to me," said Hal, thoughtfully handing Ben a purse. "She wants three new plays."

Ben weighed it in one hand, and shook his head.

Southampton sighed deeply, and handed him another purse. "There's one hundred pounds in gold, and all I have from the game last night."

Ben grinned alarmingly, stuffed both purses in a huge pock-

* *With the help of God there is nothing to be afraid of, but fools must be taught by experience.*

et, and started down the water-stairs. Then he remembered something.

"I'll need money for a horse. And horsemeat."

The Earl's sigh this time was pitiful. He found a few coins. "Thank heaven your Latin is flawless, or I'd not trust that face."

"Thank my teacher, William Camden," said Ben, and down the water-stairs he went to the softly flowing Thames.

chapter twenty-six

❧❧ EATING his way out of Middlesex from inn to inn, the classical scholar came to Harrow Hill, where he paused to drink well, and feed his new horse, and looked about the fat and smiling fields, and was glad to see such abundance of sheep, hens, chickens and hogs. As for the crops of wheat and barley, it seemed that they might this year be almost good enough to make up for the sour and mouldy harvests of the past three summers.

Who knows? he thought, pausing at Acton to feed his horse and sample the cheeses and baked meats at the good inn there. I might be a farmer myself, sometime, and buy my coat of arms, like this country Willy of theirs.

Also at Southall, and again at Uxbridge, and onward at deliberate speed out of Middlesex into Oxon and its mild and delicate air, its fertile and bounteous farms, rich in corn and cattle: the well-fed courier frequently drew rein and attended to his appetite for the good things to be offered in this healthful and happy land. At Oxford he was especially well-nourished in the Crown Inn, and his mind felt good among all the learning going about on two legs in this new Athens for the English Muses.

What a shame that I was too poor to feed upon all the learning they have here, he thought. What a pity for them that they did not know me!

Alas, poor England, with such a scholar put to so little use!

He sold his horse to John Davenant, the host at the Crown, kissed Jane Davenant, the hostess, and with the money he now had in his own pocket was able to comfort himself with fish, bacon, ham, beef, mutton, and five or six kinds of poultry; so by the time he joined a party of farmers and small dealers in wool and hides, riding a post horse, he felt quite superior to these dull cloddish men, and put a good face on the whole situation.

If I had stood for a degree at Oxford, it would have been hard for them, he thought. For who would have examined me?

When I am famous, and great, and renowned for learning, I will return to these pleasant little colleges and refresh the poor students with my wisdom.

The party of earth-bound men rode on among the beeches of Buckinghamshire, among the chalky hills and rich pastures, pausing from time to time to eat and drink together. And the unknown poet and scholar ate with them, and drank with them too, and won eight shillings and sixpence at cards.

Leaving them at Tiddington, in Warwickshire, he rode on through the green heart of England, past villages and towns, water meadows and grazing lands, until he came to the busy market town of Stratford-on-Avon.

Glaring around him at the small thatched houses on the narrow streets, and at the many shops, and the butchers' stalls, and the barrows and stands of the fat and contented merchants in Rother Street, High Street, and all up and down Middle Row on Bridge Street, the classical scholar shook his head and gave up trying to understand how any poet, play-cobbler, or strutting player could endure to live in this dull, unenlightened place, where trade and gain were the only concern, and people hated strangers, and were afraid of him.

At least five times Ben Jonson received only muttered or evasive replies when he inquired in polished and polite phrases, clauses and paragraphs for William Shakespeare, the player, playwriter and poet.

"We'll have no players here," one beady-eyed constable informed him.

"Ask at the market house," said a suspicious goodwife. "They'll find out nothing from me."

Pox on this muttering population! I would half believe that sweet Mr. Shakespeare never wrote a play, or bemused the

Queen and Court, not to speak of the fops of men of fashion! These mean narrow houses, full of darkness, with all their windows eyeing me, as if I were a murderer — how could this paragon among all wordy men who ever lived have sprung from this ignoble corner?

Of all the wonders of God, this dreaming Shakespeare is one of the strangest, and I come near losing my faith that I've ever seen the man, and heard him.

He strode into the taproom of the Bear, at the east end of Bridge Street, as far away as he could get from the mean and suspicious town, and asked for pickled beef and a decent beer if they had any.

It was in this more mellow and friendly place, after eating pretty well and drinking rather better, that Ben at last found out what was the trouble.

It was his unfortunate habit of asking too eloquently for an answer, the host whispered to him. "Ye've told 'em all too much, master," whispered the well-padded old man who presided here among the dull tradesmen at their drinking and gaming. "Why, ye ought to know that players have been outlawed here now since I myself was high bailiff. We'll not have any more plays. And Mr. Shakespeare is no player, and he hates all to do with plays. Lost his son, the very apple of his eye, on account of plays. A sad case, master. Never call him a player here, or ye'll only bring trouble to him and yourself."

Ben Jonson opened his mouth two or three times; swallowed his words; opened it again; swallowed some more; and ordered another beer for himself and one for the kind host, whose name was Barber, Tom Barber.

"That's my butcher shop right along the Middle Row," said Tom Barber, a little slow in the joints but prompt with the beer. "Do a better business than the Cawdreys ever did here. You in a trade, master? We haven't seen ye afore in these parts."

Ben swallowed quite hard, breathed deep, shook his head as if coming up out of a swamp, and answered, "The brick and

mortar trade. Mr. Shakespeare did some business with my
company. He is well, I hope?"

Tom Barber shrugged, put his old bald grey head sideways,
spread out his hands.

"I've known him, man and boy, for all his life. He has his
ups and downs. Who hasn't? He might be down now. Family
things, mostly. You know him well?"

"And love him, and loved his son, as much as ever I loved
any people in this sad world."

"Ah, now that's another subject it will be better not to bring
up with him, when ye see him, master," Tom Barber said,
nodded, shook hands, and started away to see what a party of
butchers from Nottingham might need.

"Where —?" Ben asked.

"Oh, along the river. In the woods. He takes long walks.
Sometimes all night too. Good day, master. We honoured his
father and we're learning to honour him."

"Thanks for your kind help, and your beef and beer are
good," Ben said, and in a little while he paid his shot and
started down over the bank croft to the river he saw gleaming
broad and slow beyond the feathery trees.

Someone was following him, no doubt about it. Three times
the scholarly cat-man turned around and saw a shadowy form
among the shapes and shadows of the mossy trees. Twilight
was almost at hand and the watery light of fading afternoon
presented the lurking figure to him so many shapes from his
imagination that he was amazed, when he suddenly sprang
back and caught this creature cowering behind a tree, that in
his arms he had a fair, frightened girl.

What eyes staring up at him, and such hair too! Nearly as
bright as his own. A golden dust of freckles across her nose
and comely cheeks.

"Lord, a girl!" Ben muttered, and let her go.

"I'm not afraid," she said, her chin quivering, and faced him
with her shoulders back. Great heaven of wonders, my own

dead Mary might have grown into this miracle, he thought.

The ghost of another brave and comely child danced before him in the forest shade. I know this one, he decided. The same mad courage that broke my heart.

"Heaven and the sweet angels bless thee, my child, I loved thy brother Hamnet, and I seek thy father, only for his good. Be not afraid of me. I would not hurt a child of grace, and it seems thou art his daughter Susanna."

The young girl smiled, showing uneven teeth still struggling in the small room of her winsome mouth. Older than Hamnet when he died. Why is the man in despair, with such a gift?

"And I know who you are. You're that man Hamnet liked so much he talked about you half the time he was raving in fever. My mother is afeared of you, Mr. Jonson, Mr. Benjamin Jonson. She says you shall never see my father again, if she knows it."

A damp, cold mist was rising from the broad, still river. Ben shivered and bowed his head.

"I meant no harm," he said, choking. "The country hates us now, and you may hate me too if you like. I'll go now."

Susanna ran forward and took his hand and spoke rapidly.

"Hamlet loved you, sir, as much as anyone he ever saw. And I love you, and my father loves you. If you will keep it a secret, I'll lead you straight to him."

Ben nodded his head and gently pressed her hand, not being able to speak at the moment.

"Come then," Susie whispered. He followed her deeper among the trees.

When she came to a ragged copse among larger trees, where vines trailed and hung in a thicket of alders, she stooped low and went creeping forward very cautiously. Ben got down on his hands and knees and crawled after her. A ruin of a shepherd's hut and a broken apple tree. And bees buzzing in and out, and pale yellow butterflies twinkling past his very nose.

"He's awake," Susie whispered. "See him?"

Not at first, surely. Not at all, and then the tiny patches of light among the shade suddenly added up into a form he knew.

"Now I do."

"Never tell him," Susie murmured, her eyes, hazel with flecks of gold, resting on his gravely.

"Never," whispered Ben. A slight rustle, and the girl was gone.

There sat his friend, leaning his head upon his hand, gazing into that green sea of intricate shade, like a man sunk in another world, perhaps another element, like the sea.

As if hearing something not of this world, the man in the deep green shade cocked his head, closed his eyes, and listened.

Again it came, a sound unmistakable.

Shakespeare opened his eyes and looked toward that opening between the bramble bushes from whence the golden tinkle came.

A bony, freckled hand, with warts and scars, not to mention a few scratches, was dangling a fat and well-filled purse in a narrow sun-ray.

A bad dream? A good dream?

A craggy, pockmarked face, with a hooked nose, bent sideways as from a last tweak by a vindictive sculptor, little crooked eyes winking and blinking, and a mouth grinning hard, with all possible charm.

"*Vade retro, Satanas*," Shakespeare said.

Without speaking, the devil, the satyr, or the male nymph, produced a second purse fatter than the first, and wagged them both before his friend's absent gaze.

"My Latin is getting weak," said Shakespeare.

"It is from the Queen," said Ben. "Oh, sweet friend, pity me. My feet to my head, I am all one bruise, and I ache like a bad tooth. Be kind, comfort me, and take the woman's money before she changes her mind."

Shakespeare looked gaunt and dull, and he seemed much older. His voice too was dull.

"Tempt me no more. Plate not my vanity with gold, nor weigh my shoulders with a golden yoke. Sit down with me and let us be comfortable one to another."

"Willy, Willy, forgive me my trespasses and deliver me from this evil, this golden weight of woe. How glad I am to see thee, and how damnable hard it is to do!"

"I think my girl Susie must have led thee here, thou naughty man."

"Impossible! What girl? My nose smelt thee out, in spite of all keepers, constabulls, et cetera. Willy, no words but these and then I'll creep onward, never to see thee again."

"It is words I have lost my liking for," Shakespeare said.

Ben sighed and muttered, and then with innocence enough to deceive a sneaking sheriff's man, rattled the two fat purses together before throwing them away into the bramble bushes.

Shakespeare lifted one eyebrow a little way, closed his eyes and appeared to sleep.

"Willy," Ben said. "No more, not one word more, no, no. Not about the Queen. Not about the great Earl of Essex and his great new beard. Not about Southampton, high in favour and clapped in the very bosom of the Queen. Why, he can do anything, that boy. It may be, even marry the wench. But nothing of that. Ha! We care not. What if Hunsdon is dead? And the players unprotected? And our biggest and fattest enemy, the lardy lord of the salt-marshes, is made Low Lord Chamber Pot? Pox on him! What care we if our poor ragged friends, the players, fill the prisons and the gutters? The Blackfriars playhouse, at such a cost to the Burbages, closed up for good on complaint of the householders in the neighbourhood? Mere trifles, mere nothings. James Burbage sick and impotent, the poor sons doomed to skulk the earth like unclean spirits out of mouldy graves? No, no, I am buying a big house in Hogsden Common and will fatten pigs for bacon. My last word to thee, Willy, is to do likewise. Buy thee a big fat house on a big fat street and raise fat cattle in thy orchard. There. Amen. That is my end."

Shakespeare murmured dully, "I will buy no house."

"After all, what are friends? What is friendship? Ha ha! That bosom friend of thine from Stratford signed the petition against the Blackfriars. Well, he's rich. He married the printer's widow. Let us all get rich, like Mr. Richard Field."

"We cannot do it," Shakespeare said.

"I tell thee, it will be easy. Suffer me to instruct thee. Question: What is money? A whore. Question: How to have her? Any man can have her. Question: How to buy her favours? Look at such men as have done it. I have a new way of dressing dogskins that I swear will bring me ten thousand pounds. I will do Ralegh and Essex out of their monopolies of sweet wines. How? Ha ha. By making it from raisins. And for eating? I fear thou and I have not eat enough for these three months, my ghastly friend. But when we shall, let us eat nicely, like a mincing macaroni, that is to say, with forks. Forks! From Italy! I will make a private arrangement with the linen drapers, whereby they will offer me no obstacles. For my forks will be a mighty saver of linen. Ask me not how to woo money! I shall serve the whole state with toothpicks. I will have a book printed to teach the young their use. And my many friends and admirers among the lordly shall decree that all children must learn to read, in order to apprehend the right and proper manner of picking the teeth."

Shakespeare stirred a little. He moved a leg, then another. How sadly, darkly, drably he was dressed! The common kersey of a coal boatman, or a water-carrier. No style or grace, and starred with cockleburs too, and torn here and there.

"I say no to all of it. We cannot make any money," Shakespeare said.

Ben began to swell. He trembled. His neck and face grew red.

"Why not?" he muttered.

"Because we are such fools we throw away two good purses into the bushes," Shakespeare said.

Ben burst out laughing, and then crying. He held out his arms. They embraced.

"Oh God, thou art the man I knew," he sobbed, snuffling and gulping.

"My poor Benjamin, I am no good. I do not want to live."

"Hell and sulphur, who does? It is our affliction, not our wish. I must say it, Willy. Blackfriars is pooped, because of me. Dick Field is against us, because of me. The players have given up the ghost, because of me. Henslowe is ruined, Langley is bankrupt, the playhouses closed, Topcliffe summoned back from the mountains of the North, to wrack, twist, wrench, torture poor players, because of me. Poor Mrs. Lynn has lost her hiding place in Blackfriars, because of me. The boy I loved is dead, and because of me."

"Lay not such flattering unction to thy soul," said his friend. "In this mean world there is no room for great sinners any more. This is a time for small and middle-sized men. Let us creep about among the fallen figures of our broken gods, seeking out such profit as we may make in our business. One question: What trade dost thou follow now?"

"Laying bricks," Ben mumbled.

Shakespeare breathed deep. It was deep and dusky in the dell.

"We had better find those fat purses before it is dark," he said.

Ben slapped himself upon the chest, grinned, chuckled, and then they got up and scrabbled around in the bramble bushes until they had the purses.

"All beauty does not last until autumn," Ben said, holding up a purse.

"Therefore let us enjoy our summer while it lasts," said Shakespeare, holding up the other. "How much?"

"One hundred big, beautiful pounds. I lied. It is from Southampton. He desires a little entertainment or two, for the Queen, at Christmas or before, if possible."

"Speak no more. I have whole volumes in folio for my thoughts, but I will not speak them either. I think I needed to be well thumped with the bricks of thy logic, and that these few friendly bruises hurt me well. Tell me in five words, sweet Benjamin, hast thou a horse?"

"Frankly, I have no horse."

"Then let us to the horsemarket before it closes, and pick out two good ones," said Shakespeare.

chapter twenty-seven

〰〰 NO hitch to the horse business, but the devil's own hitchings and haltings to the house business.

When the jingling Shakespeare tiptoed into the office of High Bailiff Sturley, he left the wall-eyed scholar outside the door.

"How can we move old Underhill, when his every move is noted by the priest-hunters? Tell me that, Abe."

Honest Abe Sturley kneaded his bony hands awhile. "I will put it to you, Willy, in a nutshell. How much can you pay for the tithes?"

"One hundred pounds in gold."

"Will you move your wife and daughters into the old house? And rebuild the west gable and clean out the ditch?"

"The best brickman in London shall preside over every brick. I have him here, on the threshold."

Ben Jonson, grinning with all charm possible to one with such an affliction of face, stuck in his head and bobbed it up and down.

"Very well, Willy, my boy." Abe jumped up and shook hands and was going to shake hands with Ben too, but thought better of it. A seasoned lawyer and ten-in-a-hundred man, the friendly bailiff was already enjoying the money coming to the Stratford Corporation.

"My friend Mr. Jonson and I will be riding to London to-morrow."

"All good business ride with you, and take care," Abe said. "Ah, it does me good to see your reform of conscience, Willy. Henceforth you're a sound man, a man who knows that good money comes from corn, malt, and shares in property."

"Indeed, Abe, indeed," murmured Shakespeare piously.

Alas for the cat-man's good intentions, and for such room as there might be set aside for right thinking in the reformed player's head.

"It was not money from corn, malt, or gouging tenants!" Ben suddenly blurted out. "It was a due and just reward paid in advance for three plays to be performed before your Queen and my Queen, by the name of Elizabeth, who is also Queen of this barbarous and ignorant country of England! These three plays to be played at her Majesty's Christmas Revels, where no fat-witted country justices or addled aldermen can creep in to commit castration of your Shakespeare's honestly begotten and ever-living works."

Abe Sturley dropped one purse. Shakespeare dropped the other. Stooping to pick them up, both men knocked heads.

"Yea, verily, and may more knotheads be well-knocked in this blind and brutish town!" roared Ben.

"This is the strangest bricklayer I ever did see," Abe muttered to his dazed friend.

"And may the pox take all towns that will not honour the true and worthy words of that man who stands afore ye!" continued Ben. "There breathes not in all England, not a more noble and more generous man in all England than that man there, nay, nor one better endowed by nature for this proud task, with due aid, assistance, and right counsel from certain expert advisers. Let him be honoured in the place of his birth! I say, let him be known, let him be comprehended, let him be assisted and abetted, for he has great work to do!"

Eyes glaring, face glistening, hair wildly straggling and as bright as a bonfire, the angry scholar nodded, clanked his teeth together three times, shook his fist in the air, and went out of the office and down the stairs, weeping uncontrollably, wild with rage and sorrow at the universal blindness of men, and ready to fight anybody, anywhere, for any reason or no reason at all, if one more dull, brutish, pious and deluded countryman so much as looked at him crooked.

Fortunately his vision was so dimmed by copious tears that

he made it to the Bear and the first cup of sack before he could clearly see anybody, and after that it was better.

Up in Abe Sturley's office, though, it was not so good. Shakespeare was crying; Abe was crying.

"No, no, I have sworn, it is useless, my mind is dried up, I am for malt and corn henceforth, no one can shake me."

"Now, now, Willy, not so fast, be not so hasty, there is some good in what the man said, there is no harm in *some* plays. Why, I've always liked plays, and so has Dick Quiney too, that is to say, good moral plays, Willy, good old moral plays. What! We are men, we know the world."

"No, no, they lead our youth astray," Shakespeare said gloomily, staring fatalistically straight ahead, as into a perfectly moral, wholesome future. "Well, I'll go after him with the Queen's gold and give it back to him. Corn and malt for me, Abe. No more plays, Abe, none. I am for singing some good rousing hymns, and then to the corncribs."

"Wait, Willy! Wait, man, wait! The Good Book has the answer for us, as it has for all pious men. For is not the writing of plays for the Queen herself not now duly proved and demonstrated to be your vocation? Is it not, Willy? Eh? Eh?" stammered Sturley, his nose twitching and his little eyes glittering with intelligent piety and greed.

Shakespeare cast down his eyes modestly and sighed. "Alas, it is to be admitted that her Majesty has spoken some few words of kindness for my frail fabrications."

"Well then! Well then, man! Do not give him back the money! For is it not true, is it not true, that it is no sin for a man to labour in his vocation? Tell me that, now, tell me that, Willy, but think hard, man, think hard."

Meekly concentrating on this highly soothing interpretation of Scripture, Shakespeare tried not to burst out into a howl of laughter. Great God, what a good man can twist out of holy words is a lesson to mere sinners, he thought. Composing his twitching features still further, he was able to mutter some duly chastened and seemly monosyllables that might be taken for assent.

"That's the truth of it, Willy, now that's the full truth of it, for we're men of the world. What! We have all suffered blows, we have all felt the back of Fortune's hand. Look at me and my poor wife, now, our family house burnt in the dreadful fire, my youngest boy dead, and my own poor Anne near distraction like your Anne. It is a frailty to women, Willy, and we must bear it like men. She can live in Tom Bell's good timber-framed house with us, right on the High Street, and the women can be comfortable to each other. I'll move thy affairs with Council, Willy, and before spring we'll have all accomplished. Why, my two girls love Susie and Judy, and it will be more secure for them there."

Shakespeare was ashamed of his secret laughter, and felt the tears coming again.

"Poor women," Abe added, "they are that weary of the same faces, and the same places, and the same sounds —"

Shakespeare thought of the tuneless singing of the helpful Hathaways, and the eternal talking of Dame Hathaway, and felt sudden joy, almost hope.

"Abe, forgive me for being such a burden," he said, and they clasped hands.

"Ah, that's the boy, Willy, now find thy friend, he's a good man, and tell her Majesty we're true and loyal members, and mean her no harm. So write thy plays, write them well for the Queen, and meanwhile I will move discreetly in thy affairs, in preparation for thy return. There will be the auditing, and the surveying, and the registering, and the filing of fees and fines. And then too, Willy, it might brace up thy father to have his arms, like the rest of us, for who of us all is more deserving?"

Shakespeare felt his throat ache, and instead of any more words, handed Abe the smaller of the two purses, smiled, nodded, waved his hand, and went down the stairs to find Ben Jonson.

chapter twenty-eight

〰〰 "IT is true that I can buy more medicines," the pensive horseman kept saying to the impatient one.

"Where better? Where better?"

They were passing through Garsington, followed by a swarm of blackbirds, which were scrupulously picking up every little seed left in the well-combed fields.

"And good Mrs. Sturley will be happy with Anne in a tight little house on High Street, where they can look out of windows in four directions and see the market, and hear people, and watch them all the way up, down, and across the street."

"Nothing for women has ever been known to be better."

"I can consult with Dr. Bright himself at St. Bart's. He knows the most about melancholy of anybody in all the known world."

Ben grunted. Shakespeare looked anxiously over at him, a sight to frighten a highwayman, extremely valuable as a riding companion.

"I am interested in what he observes of the air most meet for melancholic folk. He says it ought to be thin, pure and subtile, open and patent to all winds, especially to the south, and southwest. I made certain that Anne would keep the wind coming in from that corner."

Another grunt from Ben. No words, none.

"Dr. Bright observed at St. Bart's, and I think poor Lopez observed it too, that when men were maddest, they were mad north-northwest."

Ben looked suspiciously at his great and famous literary friend, who needed helpful restraint to keep him from going quite wild again with words. It was his weakness.

Shakespeare turned to him a perfectly smooth, innocent, and honest, open and candid countenance.

"I have news from Northumberland," said Ben. "The doctor

184

waxed so melancholy from much brooding upon melancholy that he resigned his post at St. Bart's, took holy orders, and is now rector at the rectory of Berwick-in-Elvet, where he preaches the hot fires of hell, feasts upon sea birds, including terns, puffins, and eider duck, drinks only good Scotch brews of proof, and for diversion, refines his art of short and secret writing, which he learned from the great Greeks, and which I will in due course teach to thee, for thy handwriting is tortured, crabbed, cramped, and inciteth the brain of man to dangerous fevers and unlawful impulses, which must be watched."

Shakespeare shrugged, and clapped heels to his horse.

In Chiselhampton village a madman was being whipped at cart's tail. Behind him leaped and danced a merry throng of boys, hooting and throwing stones. His naked back was black with blood and flies; from time to time he sank down and let himself be dragged through mud and over stones, while crying out not for mercy, but for death. Then his official healer whipped him therapeutically harder, until he rose and staggered on. At each blow a choking breath was beaten from his lungs; he twisted his poor arms, tied together at the wrists, and gnawed at the rope.

"Sweet God, give me death, death—"

His red-rimmed eyes looked at the two riders and he bared his teeth at them. The lash curled over his face, and he screamed.

The two riders spurred their horses away from that village toward the next. Soon they were on a vast bare heath, across which the wind blew fallen leaves. When they went down into the first glen the road was gone and had become a slough, in which lay a dead horse all murmurous with flies. They rode along a farmer's oat field, and then through brambles, and then through mire. It seemed near supper time, for what pale sun there was in this windy mist was searching the trees' shivering boughs from a crown of feathery furze at the horizon's rim. They heard church bells, a slow dull clang, making the heart ache and the mind sad for all those many plundered churches and those many ruins. Clouds of swift-winged swallows, feeding as they flew, went dipping and rising around and above their heads, haunted a black ruined tree awhile, and suddenly rose up twittering and were gone into dark specks and then into nothing.

"The air bites, it has a nip in it," said Ben.

"A nipping and an eager air," agreed Shakespeare.

As if their horses agreed with them, the two good animals broke into a trot. So they came in sight of a tidy group of thatched houses hugging the southeast slope of a hill. In front of a neat half-timbered cottage a woman was standing, calling her Harry to supper. A ruddy-cheeked boy, with eyes of happiness darkly bright, ran past them, crying, "Here I am, mother!"

Half chiding, half relieved, the woman seized him by the shoulders and hurried him inside, still telling him that he was late, that he had been running and playing too long.

The cottage door, and the good warmth and fragrance of the kitchen, vanished suddenly when she closed the door. Darkness now, and mist rising.

Shakespeare felt himself borne on a wave of grief so great, so powerful, that all his determined brightness of these nightmare weeks was gone. The pain overwhelmed his heart, and he wept.

"God be merciful to us all," stammered Ben, and wept with him.

A discouraged constable talked to them in a mumbling corner at Watlington's one inn, and it looked bad indeed for the country.

"Ah, bad times, bad times, my masters," said the melancholy constable, over ale and mutton and some green cheese. "Infinite number of wandering idle people, and those evil gipsies we thought we had cut off by law, again springing up. Whip 'em till my arms fall off, and still they come. Beer and

ale scarce enough, and they'll make you a brew of water and
five or six spoonfuls of annis seed. Corn's so dear, we make
our bread out of cuckoopit or pompions, and a man's belly
rumbles from morn till night. Our children growing up that
thin and starved it's a wonder they live. What's to become of
the country with these wandering sojers in all the shires?
Send 'em all off again, I would, and I'd tell the Queen so too,
if I ever saw her. Send half of the idle worthless fellows to
Ireland and put down those savages for good, I would. Send
the other half to France, and let 'em kill the Spanishers there,
before they land on our coasts, that's what I'd do. Peas and
beans all spoilt too. Hay mouldy and makes the cows' bellies
swell up. This country's gone bad, it has, and our younkers no
good any more either. All running off to the plays and the
alehouses and the bawdy houses, eh? Prices going up all the
time. More ale, masters? A windy night coming."

"Thank you, master, but we'll ride to High Wycombe before we rest," said Shakespeare, and on they went again.

"This melancholy is more a plague than the pox or the
blight or the tertian fever," Ben muttered between his horse's
ears.

"Poverty and want, servitude and sorrow, vain fears, abuses,
contempts, contumelies and scorns," said Shakespeare, in a
voice like music.

"We must put a good face upon this affliction of living, or
the poor Queen will scream. A comedy first, to cheer up her
flagging spirits? Every courtier I saw when I was called to
Richmond had the black melancholy worse than another. It
is our time's disease, I do believe."

"Perhaps a history?" said Shakespeare. "There is a clang of
arms and the bray of trumpets in my head."

"What, again?" said Ben.

"The more is England idle, restless, weary, jaded and uncertain with this peace, the louder we should shout of her
glories in old wars. I think I feel a history coming."

"It is not correct," Ben said. "Three rusty swords, a heap of
words a foot long, or half a foot, and false wounds painted on

in the tiring house? Has the man not learned? Has the man not profited? Will the man not see?"

Shakespeare was as patient with the classical scholar as he could possibly be, and yet he was becoming peopled with an old head-population he thought had been evicted.

Like the swooping swallows, the twittering creatures of the winds, his familiar friends, namely, words, in flocks of long beautiful speeches, came swarming back to him; and he heard the far-off music of happiness.

He shivered, but not with cold. His eyes sparkled, his nostrils dilated, and he tossed his head like a high-mettled horse.

Words, words, words, words!

If nothing else will cure this pestiferous melancholy in which all England wallows as in a bog, let me have words to speak her glory, and I will ask no more.

And for all the rest of the aching journey he listened only a little to the man of classical rules and complicated humours, for he heard a secret music. And no matter how many ragged wanderers, blighted beadles, cranky constables, ruined yeomen, or sorrowful businessmen muttered their woe on muddy roads or in mouldy inns, his heart remembered his one great joy, and his own fears and sorrows were mended.

But the nights were long and dark, and it was then that the spirit of his dead son returned to him, and he could neither sleep nor rest. Grief filled up the room, lay in his bed, walked up and down with him. And the whole world was not enough when he heard the voice of his absent child speaking to him in the dark night of the soul.

Are you sick, father? You look sad tonight. Let me sit all night and watch with you. I think I love you more then you do me.

The glimmering day would find him on his knees.

Ah God, never may I taste again the pleasures of the world, never be infected with delight, never know ease and idleness, until I have set a glory in this land.

chapter twenty-nine

〰〰 THE play was almost done. Even the bawds and hawkers in the pit were silent, and the fops had not stirred from their stools on the stage for an hour.

Under the open sky, with the low sun flashing on their copper lace and crimson, the victorious king, princes, lords and knights paraded before the thronging galleries, while the rebels were led off to execution. The new play of *Henry IV* was a triumph already at Court, and now it was setting the galleries in a roar.

Dick Burbage, the heroic Prince Henry, stepped forward to receive the applause.

But what was this shouting from the galleries and from the pit?

"Falstaff! Bring back Falstaff! We want the fat knight! Falstaff! Falstaff!"

They were chanting it now, and stamping.

"Falstaff! Falstaff! More Falstaff!"

Shakespeare, disguised as King Henry, and Nick Tooley, as Lord John of Lancaster, stood there in the brightness while the cheers and shouts grew more noisy and insistent.

So there came rolling and limping in a gross fat man with a white beard and a bald head, grinning and waving a bottle of sack, old Tom Pope the very model of that great new mocker of morality, that monstrous coward and sinner, that drinker and wencher, that thief, that grey iniquity, that father ruffian, that swollen parcel of dropsies, that wool-sack, that bed-presser, that huge hill of flesh, with no more faith in him than in a stewed prune in a bawdy house — Falstaff, the fat-witted knight who corrupted youth and was able to corrupt a saint.

Such a roaring yell went up to the smoky sunset, and off over the chimney pots of Southwark, as had never been heard on Bankside in living memory.

"Damn thee, Willy, I thought I was the hero of this piece," muttered Burbage, itching in his armour and smiling a sickly painted smile.

"Alas, so did I," muttered the repentant Shakespeare.

Sweat was dripping from old Tom Pope as he danced and laughed, jigged and bowed, waved and blew kisses to the screaming galleries. As for the fashionable fops who had seen the wonders and glories of Shrewsbury, the death of Hotspur, and the rout of Douglas and Glendower, they were being engulfed by the strong-smelling groundlings from the pit, who had now climbed up onto the stage and were dancing around Tom Pope, the new hero of the low and the high, the gentlemen and businessmen, the fine ladies and the dolls of the quarter, not to mention the great Queen Elizabeth, who had shouted with laughter on the mighty night when Falstaff first asked Prince Hal the time of day at the Boar's Head Tavern in Eastcheap.

"Oh God, and we were going to give old Tom Pope the sack," Dick Burbage groaned. "Now we'll never be rid of the old bastard."

Shakespeare looked suitably chastened by this remark from his rich and powerful partner, who was certainly the next-greatest actor in England, if not already the greatest.

"Dick, I meant this play to be all about honour, glory, triumph, order and justice," he murmured sadly, "but something came between my intention and my execution, and I fear we have begotten another whoreson comedy."

It was hopeless, it was just as the indignant and eloquent Ben Jonson hotly declared five or six times to anybody who would listen, and also to fifty or sixty rapidly departing people who would be damned if they would listen — this Shakespeare would mock at every reverend virtue with a still more reverend vice, would parade his kings and earls and bishops before the galleries and then bring on such low and bawdy knaves, such rude and sinful clowns, given to all manner of bad behaviour and irreverence, that honour came limping off the battlefield while laughter, havoc and confusion danced and made merry. How could this happen, in such weighty plays, full of such noble sayings, and such airy, fiery, flowery words, fit to make people cry for sheer wonder that English could be so beautiful?

Alas, look at Tom Pope, riding upon the shoulders of twenty staggering apprentices, while noisy watermen and boiler-makers, oyster-sellers and slaughterers, cavorted across the stage that had been intended to show England her glory! There was nobody on the stage, nobody in the tiring house, nobody afterwards at the Swan on Fish Street or the Mermaid on Bread Street, who had the words, the breath, the time, the patience to explain to the thoughtful Shakespeare, and anyhow he was surrounded by so many admiring gallants and lawyers from Inns of Court that men of discretion and fears for the future of order and propriety in England could hardly get near him that night of the Fat Knight's triumph.

Where the devil did I get this Falstaff, come to think of it? Shakespeare wondered, politely answering the pleasant speeches of these men who crowded around him.

I thought he was just a last patching-up of Oldcastle in that horrible play, *The Famous Victories of Henry V*, a mere clown, a fellow they called Jockey, who robbed honest travellers on the public highway, and was meant to be hanged.

It is true that Lord Cobham made such a mighty stink at Court over calling my fat man Oldcastle, after his wife's ancestor, that I quickly dubbed him Falstaff, but what did I mean by *that* name?

How did *he* ever swell to these proportions? Great God, where and when will his swelling stop? Her Majesty has already commanded me to produce a second play of bogus history and questionable morals, to let Jack Falstaff trot again, and all my noble purposes and grave intentions are pooped by a meaty monster with no good in him.

chapter thirty

PERHAPS the Queen might have stopped it. But when the second part of *Henry IV* was performed to roars of joy at Whitehall, her Majesty jumped for glee and clapped her hands.

"Sweet Mr. Shakespeare! Witty Mr. Shakespeare! Next you must show me Falstaff in love!"

Alas, my monstrous fat man will lead me on such a dance I fear that all my good intentions will be squashed, the puzzled Shakespeare thought.

But when can I begin to give these giddy people glory? When will the Queen permit me to teach her people to be great and good?

Alas, I fear that even the preachers must sweat and grunt beneath such a grave burden. And as for myself, when I am most moral in my maxims, and most upright in my preachings, the more my silly audiences nod and gape, and the fops and stinkards alike cry out for riot, disorder, lechery and beastliness.

He asked Ben Jonson what to do about it, and was much disappointed.

"No, no, no," the classical scholar told him. "Do not spoil this peculiar popularity thou hast somehow gotten, begotten, or, as I rightly think, misbegotten. What thou must do, my boy, is give 'em more Falstaff, that's what they want. Who cares?"

Shakespeare looked at his wild-haired and pockmarked friend with gentle reproach.

"It is true that plays are nothing, and when I am gone there will not remain any more breath from these poor homunculi I trifle with," he admitted. "But my plans are to take all my profits from the company before the good men of the City and the grave men of the Privy Council chase us from our playhouses for the sixth and last time. And I have my house chosen, and my two barns, and my granary, and my brewing-house, and my good stout wall around my property, and there are some good sound investments to make with Henry Jackson and George Reynolds and Jack Combe too, which will pay off in good time. My old age creeps upon me, and I will soon be ready to depart. So one last fling at the dice of Fortune, Ben, with a noble and weighty tragedy, teaching my countrymen the vanity of joy and the evil of gluttony, not to mention civil disorders and lechery, which I fear will ever be a problem —"

"Bah!" said Ben, reaching suddenly up and sitting the moody Shakespeare down upon the padded bench beside him. "Take up thy tools! Here, now thy glass is full! Eat, man, eat! Look how thou art wasting away, while before thy very orbs this trunk of mine waxes fat!"

It was true; the man spoke nothing but truth.

Shakespeare began eating and drinking beside his learned friend, still somewhat hopeful that this well-educated man would instruct him in the right and proper ways by which he might do battle with that devil lechery, who always came between him and his grave and moral intentions.

"Eat, man, eat!" cried the man of learning. "Some foolish gudgeon for thee, mad wag! Ah, and sole too, immortal footprint of the god of fishes! Take up thy eating tools, for truly man is doomed to suffering and long toil; few indeed are his blessings, and fleeting his joys —"

"I wish that you would preach to me, Ben. I need it," Shakespeare said.

"What's the matter? Thy affairs wag well, and all England will laugh with thee in the end. Thy wife and pretty ones are well bestowed until thy great house is ready, and the worthy aldermen are waiting for thee with itching fingers, to help thee to good investments of thy well-begotten riches. Alas, if only my wife were as gentle as your Anne!"

Shakespeare looked sadly at him. "Has she beaten in thy ears again?"

"Alas, worse! She's in church, praying for strength. What

will I do if God grants her any more? Well, she may be a shrew, but she's honest. So have some sole, my poor fashionable friend, my unfortunate slave of the people's folly and the Queen's taste, and I will preach to thee."

"Good, good, I need it," Shakespeare said meekly.

"Very well! Listen, then, and profit. I have decided that it is idle to instruct the shrimp in the art of whistling, and the crow in the beauty of ordered harmony. I have been wrong in attempting to instruct thy rude, barbarian wit in the airs and graces of classical comedy. No! Every man to his humour! Build thy wild and wobbly castles of a hundred towers, spires, gables, in which uncommon murders are committed, and ghouls gibber, and riot and luxury caper pell-mell, with an infant born in one scene a full-grown man in the next, and an action begun in Greece wandering all over Africa and Egypt before this monstrous pageant is ended with a riot in Rome. The Lord of Misrule learn order and decorum? It is against nature, and I am the first to point out this great truth to all that will hear my words. Here is a man, ye gods, in whose one English head boils and bubbles Oriental heat and planetary fire. Who will hold him back? Who will hold him down?"

The polite listener waited with some interest to learn the answer.

"That man's a fool who would temper thy equinoctial winds with the calmness and reason of antipodial intellection. And no such a man am I. Henceforth my mission is clear. I shall reform the thick and dark ignorance of this pestilential age, but I shall not any longer attempt to do this by instructing the perturbed spirits of our time in the true art of dramatic construction. How shall I do this? Do I hear a voice inquiring how?"

"I rise to inquire, how?" Shakespeare remarked helpfully.

"Thanks for your request for enlightenment. My answer shall be fully given in the form of a correct and classical comedy, in five acts, a prologue explaining and expounding the action to follow, and an epilogue recapitulating and clarifying the moral lessons illustrated and illuminated in each orderly and logical scene. My fame from this badly needed comedy shall be blown abroad on the wings of the wind, I shall be exalted and flattered by those who now caper after every ape of form and ass of fashion, and so shall England be enlightened, instructed, and improved, all in one excellent classical bundle. Will this not be marvellous? Say, will this be so, or will it not be so? I pause for the answer."

"It will be so, it shall be so, and God grant it may be so and so," answered Shakespeare. "May one of the vulgar be so crude as to inquire what this marvel shall be named?"

"You may well and truly inquire, and I will well and truly reply. It shall be called *Every Man in His Humour.*"

Little Francis, the tapster's boy, hearing the clang of Shakespeare's spoon beating applause upon his trencher, came running in to see what was wanted.

"Huffcap for the gentleman in the padded breeches," said the one in blue and silver, with the eyes so merry and yet so sad. "And mad dog and angel's food for me. For a day is coming that we wot not of, and the like of which no man hath seen."

chapter thirty-one

〰〰 WHILE England waited the day, and knew it not, the dark and ignorant country made the best of its condition by suddenly bestowing upon one rude and untutoured son two or three random rewards for which he no longer had any stomach.

Item, to one William Shakespeare, player, upon long and fruitful consideration by Garter King at Arms and the due solicitation and advice of Clarenceux William Camden, of the College of Heralds, one handsomely emblazoned pattern, on parchment, suitably illuminated and appropriately tinted, of one coat of arms for the honourable and rightful use of one man of worship, namely, that grave and substantial citizen, John Shakespeare, hereafter and forever to be known as gentleman, of Stratford-upon-Avon, in the county of Warwick, to bear and use the same, single or impaled, during his natural life, and for his children, issue, and posterity to bear, use, and quarter, and show forth the same, a coat as follows:

In a field of Gould uppon a Bend Sables, A Speare of the first the poynt upward hedded Argent, and for his creast or cognizance A Falcon, with the wynges displayed, standing on a wrethe of his coullers Supporting a Speare Armed hedded or & steeled sylvor fixed uppon a helmet with mantelles & tasselles.

The herald handed over the parchment to that gentle, quiet man standing there in the golden glimmer from the mullioned window of the Mermaid, in Bread Street, took his fee, wished the newly created gentleman good day, and departed.

A shudder went over the figure in modest blue and silver, which was the household livery of Robert Dudley, the Earl of

Essex, and it appeared that for a moment Mr. Shakespeare was feeling ill.

But he poured himself a cup of wine with a shaking hand, turned again toward the window looking on Cheapside, raised the cup and whispered a toast which no living ears might hear, for it was addressed to one dead and cold, whose lovely eyes and lips were blind and silent forever.

And when he had drunk the wine, he smashed the cup to pieces on the hearth.

He then put on his hat and cloak, looked to his sword and pistols, whistled for Francis, paid him for bread, cheese, beef, wine, and one broken cup, and then went out to the stable-yard and called for his fine horse, to ride to his fine master, or at least his temporary master, that same Earl of Essex who was the most brilliant ascending star in the Court of England.

He paid the ostler well and was on his way to Westminster, in order to be well noted and well remarked among the followers of the well-favoured and generous young Earl. The reason for such conspicuity being entirely clear to all and several witnesses of the thumps and clouts, not to say kicks, lately bestowed upon the late players of the late Lord Hunsdon, now the players of nobody at all, and therefore vulnerable to all blows that might happen to fall upon them, or be directed to strike upon them and beat them down, by that gross fat man now dignified by the title of Lord Chamberlain, namely the beastly and brutish William Brooke, the seventh Lord Cobham, also a favourite of the giddy Queen, with the power to banish, disallow, inhibit, put down, and quite extinguish those men of small worth and little light, namely, players.

Which this loutish lord was lately proceeding to begin, at his pleasure and leisure, to do.

So it was at Westminster, where the newly created gentleman was too deeply absorbed in thought to be aware at first that his name was being called, that the second of Lady Fortune's gifts fell into his lap, in the courtyard of the Queen's

Bench, quite as if that strumpet had marked him as a man to be favoured with that useful piece of property, namely, a house.

"Mr. Shakespeare, master, we've been looking for you high and low. Here's this deed to sign and witness and be registered before the court of deeds and conveyances, for this house that's waiting this long time for you to come and claim it. Will you please to dismount and follow me in directly, Mr. Shakespeare, sir? Here, fellow, take the gentleman's horse. This way, if you please, Mr. Shakespeare, sir."

Oh God, that great and lonely pile of brick for which I peddled my soul and honour, in order that my darling, my pride, my golden boy, might hold his head as high as any gentleman of the kingdom, and be immune to Fortune's kicks and blows!

New Place, on Dead Lane, for one whose name shall die with him!

As he followed the clerk of the court of record along the narrow passageway and up the worn steps to the court of conveyances, fines and lawful penalties, he tasted a bitterness of grief once more with which he was becoming well acquainted.

chapter thirty-two

HE stood in the ragged garden of old Sir Hugh Clopton's house and let Mr. Underhill's boy turn the brass key in the lock of the big front door.

The rooks were cawing in the lime trees, the sedge warbler was twittering to his mate; and somewhere, somewhere among his own trees he heard an echo, not a voice, a faint, yet clear and unmistakable sound —

Cuckoo, cuckoo, cuckoo!

With a horrible grating noise, the door opened. They stood there, hesitating, and then Shakespeare awakened out of his dream and thanked Mr. Underhill's boy, who was named Hercules, and would be sixteen this June.

"Thank you, Hercules. We'll open the house tomorrow," he said. "Too bad your father had the cramp, and could not come."

"He often does," Hercules murmured. A quiet boy, patient and a little sad; not like the elder brother Fulke, grinning and chuckling over his idiot fancies.

"We'll open all the shutters, mend all the panes, and begin repairs directly. Much to do."

"You'll have apples from those trees," Hercules said, as the new owner pulled the door shut again and locked it with his key.

"Oh, it will be a fine garden. There will be enough to keep me busy every minute."

They walked back along the weedy path to the gate in the brick wall, which needed repairing.

A pity I did not ask Ben the true classical way of laying bricks, he thought, standing there under the bearded, mossy trees, looking up at his big looming house with its five gables, its three stories nearly covered with ancient ivy.

199

He heard the chirrup of the boy to his horse, or his father's horse, and the sudden gallop of the animal away from there, toward the bridge.

In this veiled light, under a darkening sky, the old house loomed very dark.

I'll plant grapevines all along this western wall, he thought. And mulberry trees, and new grass. Abe will give me vine sets, perhaps.

A load or two of stone, to make all square and secure. The trees all need pruning, but too late this year. The sap is running, the birds are busy, and hark to old Alexander Aspinall calling Mrs. Aspinall from the brewhouse!

Weedy ground, but very good ground, if it be well manured.

He turned three times to look back at the ranked gables of his astonishing house, then rode on up Chapel Street among the early-evening people, to Abe Sturley's house in the High Street, where Anne and his daughters would be waiting for him.

Quite a few citizens stopped to greet him, and to wish him a happy homecoming.

God grant it, though I do not deserve it, he thought, feeling himself trembling. The evening fog was in his throat.

Two young girls whispering and peeking out at them from the hedges, as the new householder, and his wife, went out early the next morning to inspect their new home. Anne saw Susie and Judy among the roses and the fallen leaves; she told them to go back. Their father saw them, and smiled indulgently.

"Good morrow, Mr. Shakespeare, sir. And Anne . . ."

They returned the morning greetings, and went on down Chapel Lane until they came to the gate in the crumbling wall. Here he stopped, took out the key, and with some persuasion got the gate open.

Anne was quiet as they went through the ragged garden, so long neglected. And what of it? Had she ever been noisy?

Ever in a rage? Ever screamed with laughter, shouted with joy, moaned with pain?

Not to me, not to me.

Perhaps alone, deep in the woods, on one of those long walks Susie told me she has been taking. Always alone and secret. But very much better in spirit. Why, she even smiled with kindness, and some joy, when at last we were alone, last night, and placed my head on her bosom.

Like a forgiven sinner, or an erring son.

Well, she's past forty, and in her climacteric.

Enough of these things. We have many cares to concern us, all good, weighty, solid cares, of timber, bricks, mortar, jars, ewers, basins, planks, beds, tables, trestles, plate, bowls, a whole universe in little, and our own, to shut us in from the moon, the stars and enemy planets.

This bush must be trimmed, he thought. A rabbit, a lame rabbit, limped out of it, became an upright rabbit, very like a little man sitting in front of his house.

"Oh, Willy, we'll have company!" said Anne, and clapped her hands.

He laughed with such relief it brought the tears to his eyes.

Thank God, thank God, for the friendship of small creatures and a ragged bush, and its small lame citizen.

Like me, he remembered. I go lame even now, when I've ridden too hard, or tired myself in some part too full of windmill gestures and the great breeze of vain words.

No more of that.

Let the floor of this house be my only stage, for the rest of my life. And the part of this householder my only study.

He put the large brass key in the lock, and turned it. He lifted the heavy brass handle, helping the tall door to open with only a small creaking and a little scraping. Mend that first. Old Tom Fossicar, if he still lives, could mend all the locks and oil them for me . . .

Anne was leaning forward, looking timidly into the darkness of this great house, this enormous great house for a shepherd's daughter, who had never had a home of her own, only other people's chimney corners.

"Oh, it's mouldy! Smell the mould," she said.

"I forgot to bring tools, in case the shutters will not open."

Well, so we enter our great house. Oh, my windy words, for the entrances of my kings and queens! Where are they now?

Nevertheless, they entered the dark and mouldy house, and were watchful because of mice, crickets, spiders, while the sound of their careful footsteps echoed from room to room. The damp and heavy air floated about them like mist; the dark rooms exhaled their musty odours, as of moss, deep woods, old leaves and rotten rushes. Indeed the shreds of old rushes lay on the floor and clung to the walls, where ghostly breezes may have blown them.

They walked on, making echoes under the great black beams of the ceiling in the galleries, the halls, the parlours, the dining room, and now the kitchen, where Anne became more at home.

Tall cupboards, wide high windows, most of their small diamond panes still sound, unbroken; a great stone hearth, and good oaken floors still.

In one cupboard he discovered a broom, in another a cracked pot, and on a bookshelf in what should be his study, a treatise on something with many syllables, in Latin.

He got a pair of shutters open, flung them apart. In poured the blessed sun, and Anne cried out in pleased surprise.

A sleepy wasp, deprived of his snug home, buzzed out and began knocking himself about the room, while Anne ran back to the kitchen for the broom.

The sun streamed in, while the rare window in the cloud-bank remained open, and he saw the tower of the gild chapel like a cardboard tower on a stage. He leaned on the sill of his study window, and heard the drowsy voices of the boys in the grammar school reciting their first lessons.

And now they were singing. He could just catch the tune,

that of an old psalm he had sung within those walls. The words floated out from somewhere in his mind, and if he closed his eyes on the shimmering scene it was gone, taking the years with it, and he was a drowsy boy again, imprisoned in the schoolroom and in the endless round of hymns and Latin lessons, dreaming of freedom, and the great world beyond these narrow walls, and all the marvels in it.

He put his hands to his face, and wept.

When Anne returned with the broom he was very busy about some cracks in the wainscoting, and when he could speak again it was about wood, nails, oil and iron to be bought from Mr. Higges, to mend things. "We'll need the best carpenter in town, and painters, plasterers, a bricklayer, an ironmonger —"

"That's Tom Smith then," his wife said, "if we can get him."

"And you'll need a cook, and a maidservant, and a gardener."

Anne's clear grey eyes looked at him in astonishment and some fear.

"Oh, what could I ever tell them? They'd laugh at me."

And indeed laughter was pealing up at them from the garden now, but it was Susie and Judy, seeing their parents there in the window, as big as life, and almost real and convincing, but not quite.

"Come up here, come up and see your new home!" he called to his daughters.

"Of course you must have servants now — you're a woman of substance, a lady with a great place to run — New Place, for Mrs. Shakespeare," he said rapidly, but the girls were running and laughing in the hall, now in the parlour, the pantry, the buttery, the dining room, back into the wing where more unnamed, unknown rooms waited for new owners, the sound of their gay voices running like a stream of new life through his galleries, his study, through the great chamber and the little chamber, and now suddenly, with fresh surprise and shrieks of joy, into the kitchen, where the two wildly excited girls could also put their tender arms and elbows on a window sill, like grown-up people, and look with tremendous dignity out into the back garden and the ragged orchard. They were putting on a show now; it was Mrs. Cloppyton and Mrs. Poppyton conversing in high exalted voices, with such airs and graces, about the terrible great cares they had, with these husbands of theirs, and these naughty, naughty children.

The father and mother silently watched them at their performance, and it was the father who was amazed, and had no words for it. But he listened to everything, as if he needed to hear more, and then more again, until he had learned the melody and made it his own.

Could this be the music of happiness?

chapter thirty-three

≫≫ AND were these his stern and upright countrymen, the grave aldermen and burgesses of Stratford, now cheerfully disposed upon padded benches at the Swan, and turning their beaming countenances toward the new householder and tithe-payer of Chapel Lane, while good old Abe Sturley proposed a toast?

"Let us now drink to our loving countryman, at home in Court and City, honoured at our ancient and holy seats of learning, in both Oxford and Cambridge, master playwright of her Majesty, by the grace of God, Queen Elizabeth — gentlemen, I give you our one, our only Willy Shakespeare!"

What, Dick Quiney, Tom Barber, Henry Wilson, Jack Gibbs, John Smith, even Tom Rogers and John Sadler on their feet and cheering?

Before the amazed householder could mutter in reply that he had put all that behind him, that he had done with writing plays, or with playing in them either, the amazing Abraham, who had married in as much haste, in the forbidden season of Advent, as the new householder had, and for the same reason, added a bit of news.

"And now it is my honour and privilege to tell our famous and distinguished friend and brother of a surprise we have in store for him and all his fellows. This afternoon, by vote of the Stratford Corporation, we have as loyal subjects of her Majesty, Queen Elizabeth, after due and grave deliberation and consideration of what is seemly and of right example for our borough and its lawful and obedient citizens, and against the examples of other well-governed cities and boroughs, held, concluded, voted, decided, and are now contented to order the performance of such plays in our hall, and in our innyards, and such other places as may be duly prepared within the town limits, as our loving countryman William Shakespeare may desire his fellows, and any others, so to perform before

205

us and all our citizens. And this to hold until the next common council, and from thenceforth forever, except as may be then finally revoked and be made void, so let's have thy plays, Willy, we're right proud and glad to see thy plays in this parish," Abe finished, coming up to Shakespeare and embracing him, while the ruddy councilmen applauded as if they were an audience, and in a playhouse already.

The honoured and well-beloved householder would close his eyes, mutter an incantation, and open them cautiously. No, his green and flourishing garden was still here. From the open windows came the sound of laughter, and the fresh voices of his daughters twittering away like a pair of wrens at their nest-building. And they would be out catching husbands in a few years, and would need good dowries.

The very air seemed throbbing with expectation. And here in the garden, breathing it, a finished, an ended man.

With no scholarly cat-man, no classical bricklayer to supervise the mending of this crumbled wall, this crooked gable. Two loads of stone, the lovely golden Cotswold stone, and a pile of goodly kiln-dried oak, with ash for new thresholds in correct imitation of the Greeks when they built houses. The odoriferous and vulgar breath of Dead Lane Ditch quite stopped and a trickling stream new-installed upon its ordered course to the Avon. And as for that name, it was Dead Lane no more, but Chapel Lane again, by grace of Act of Council, as it had been in old time and was now forever.

Two dozen ivy sets in earth, well watered: the early-rising householder came out and eyed them every morning while the dews of night still wet them, to spy out any sweet new tenderness of green. The gooseberries, the pome-waters, the bitter-sweetings would do well. No worm yet ate into the heart of any rose.

I am content. Who says I am not content?

Let any man dare stir dead leaves that hide my heart.

chapter thirty-four

〰〰 "WILLY, for the love you once bore us, at least have the grace to listen!"

Brother Ned, of all unwelcome people, haranguing him in his own private garden. The wanton Ned, in who knows what bosom of what family, hastily returned to pester a man who would be forgotten.

"My memory sleeps and will not be wakened. Have some of my honeycomb swish. It will be good for that cough."

"This is the last call, Willy. We're done."

"Call Essex. Whistle him."

Ned made an elaborate show of thoroughly fraudulent patience. "I have news of him too. He's dropped us flat. There's nobody for us, nobody."

"Chirp at Southampton. He loves birdy-boys."

"Damn this wet grass! Everything's wet here. Essex has set his face toward Ireland to end rebellion there forever, and your silly Southampton will go with him. I say there's nobody for us, unless someone, I say someone who cares —"

"I'll write you a letter. At what wench's house this time? I must confer with stonemasons this afternoon."

"You remember her. Marie Mountjoy's."

Shakespeare did not move an eyelid.

"Willy? Are you my brother? That is all."

"And more than nature herself could have expected. Give Marie a kiss but beware of the next man who passes her in the street. Her husband is no matter."

Ned eyed him with the wild, superior scorn of youth. "Who cares about the men? It's her daughter worries me more, not to speak of Joan."

Shakespeare bestowed upon this wanton boy a mild look of distaste.

"Who's Joan? The tapster's girl?"

207

"Sleeps in the shed back of Mountjoy's coalhouse."

A silence in the orchard of New Place. Thank the Lord that Anne had gone to market, taking the girls with her.

Elder Brother rose with all his dignity intact. Little Brother, already taller than he was, kicked at a mouldy tree stump.

"Everything's falling down in this place. Why all these old, old houses? Tear 'em all down I say, like the Burbages' Theatre."

A wary glance from the speaker, to the listener. Did he listen?

Shakespeare nodded in pleasant agreement.

"What I always told Dick."

"Oh, you did."

"Five years ago. People do not listen."

"Oh, hell, Willy, I'm going back and let Cobham put me in prison like Ben Jonson. Who cares what happens now? Our patrons, gone to Ireland. The only playhouse we had left to us, torn down. The most correct comedy ever written by a complete and correct man now at the mercy of every man's humour, with no place to open, and no one to play the two best parts, Lorenzo or Brainworm. I hate to see a man cry, but there it is. Well, goodbye, Willy. Me for Newgate Prison, where at least I'll have friendship."

And with a twisted smile, wiping away an imaginary tear from his right eye, Ned clasped his brother's hand and started off fast.

"Hey! Let go!" he cried, sprawling in the wet mossy grass. Shakespeare sat on him.

"Help! Help! Damn my brother for a sneak! A low acrobat with falling hair and tricky feet!"

"I'll let you in the coalhouse until we've washed you and dressed you in new breeches. Then you may proceed to the kitchen, but if you kiss my cook I'll feed you on tar and grease. You may sleep in my second-best bed provided you drag no drab in with you from Swine Lane."

"Up, up. Let me up!"

"First, why is Ben in Newgate Prison? Second, why is Tom Pope not playing Lorenzo and Will Kemp not playing Brain-worm? I gave strict orders to both."

Idiot laughter from the wet brother below.

"Tell me, or I twist this."

"Stop it, Willy! Oh, damn your ears and fingers! One of Ben's best friends from Henslowe's flock dined and drank with him to celebrate *Every Man in His Humour* at last reaching the boards, and poor Gabriel inadvertently, in commenting upon women, as men will together —"

"Yes! Yes! Onward, onward!"

"To put it in a mouldy nutshell, curse you, Gabriel Spencer insulted Ben's taste in women, including his wife."

"Then what! Then what?"

"Why, no man will stand that, a pox on you! Ben challenged him, met him in Hogsden Field, and after three parries and a tierce, swick, swack, ugh! Ran him through."

"Oh, God, he is fated. It is doom. And is Gabriel dead?"

"As mutton. Now let me up, please, Willy."

"Who dared change my orders to the company? Where is Tom Pope? Where is Will Kemp?"

"Both out and away, and good riddance I say. Kemp says he'll dance from London to Norwich before he'll be cramped in any more crooked jests by a man with his face full of holes and his wit all leaked out of his ears. Oh, I'm dying. To hell with anybody with bad manners. Oh, how vulgar are these country knaves, who have nowhere to sit but upon innocent people."

Shakespeare arose and helped his brother up. He put his arm around him and helped him limp into the house.

chapter thirty-five

〰〰 "ALAS, Willy, your news is bad," said honest Abe Sturley, kneading away at his knobby hands. "What will you do?"

A countenance innocent of all plans was turned trustfully
toward him. Outside on the stairs the uneasy Ned was mumbling and creaking.

"Who knows what anyone can do?" sighed Shakespeare.

"Who's that on my stairs? You out there, what business are
you?"

Elder Brother spoke soothingly, throwing it away: "Only
one of my brothers."

Abe was nervous today, full of carwhitchets as he called
them. "Oh, to be a man like you, with no cares but good ones,
worthy ones, like bricks and timber, corn and malt. My wife
rode me all night like that witch queen in your play, Willy.
This thing I did wrong, that thing I did not do at all. Oh,
people do not know the half of what a man goes through,
night and day, night and day. And now this murder in
Fillongley."

"Fillongley!" cried Shakespeare. "Who?"

"I was coming to that," Abe said, kneading hard again. "It
may hold back the final conveyances to your house, Willy.
We've got Phil Rogers under questioning and witnesses saw
the killer sneaking in and out of his apothecary shop. Bought
enough rat poison to kill half a village, and dosed his poor
father with it before I'd got his signature to the last writ of
assignment and surrender. Well, it happens here all the time.
Not like this in our fathers' days."

"True and sad, Abe, but who killed his father? Not —"

Abe nodded glumly and looked out the window. Across the
quad the captive children were making the air plaintive with
a hymn:

Turn . . . our . . . captivity . . .
As a br-ook in . . . the . . . south . . .

"A bad thing for a man to marry his cousin, Willy. Underhill took her for money, as a man will do. But the issue of such a marriage is already flawed, and the first was the worst. I remember I said it to more than one, that Fulke will be the death of him that begat him against the law of God."

"I hope he died quickly," Shakespeare said.

"He died every day." Abe got up to peer out into the hall. "Oh, it's you, then, Ned Shakespeare," he said. "Wait for us downstairs. No, best wait at the Bear. We'll have a drink on something or other." He came back and sat down heavily at his littered, dusty desk.

"They'll squeeze it out of him at the torture," he said. "That last paper was the most important too, Willy. Now it may have to wait a long, long time."

"How long, Abe?"

"A long, long, long time," Abe said, putting his fingers neatly together in a careful legal tent, such as a practised lawyer builds at the peroration, before admiring auditors. "Maybe till young Hercules comes of age in 1602."

All careful serenity vanished from the Shakespeare countenance.

"My wife! My daughters! My apple trees!"

"There now, Willy, I see you're a man of feeling, like myself. It does you real honour, real honour, man. Well, I'll keep on the case from time to time, until we have it in our hands, duly witnessed, signed, and filed at Westminster. Write me after you've got these things straightened and smoothed in London. If I have news, I'll send to you there in Shoreditch, will that do? Calm thyself, Willy, these things happen here all the time, as things are nowadays."

"Murder! Parricide most foul! A deed done by an idiot! Oh, the very air trembles at it! What will my poor chicks do now? No roof again? No house? No garden?"

"Why, nobody's going to trouble them where they are, Willy, unless it might be old Mrs. Hathaway come to call and stay a fortnight. It's their house, duly signed and paid to the proper owner while he lived, and the idiot son will be hanged in Warwick before three weeks are up. Nobody will contest it then. So be easy, Willy, calm thyself, man, and let us have a little merry at the Bear, and talk of London and the plays. So your fellows have lost another theatre, eh? What will they do?"

Shakespeare shuddered as though in a windstorm on Ingon Heath. He spoke quietly and reasonably.

"Let us first inquire of my well-informed brother Edmund, who will already be three drinks beyond us if we do not hurry, as to the full and horrible details, before we try the hazard of any guessing at what any man or men will do."

Young Neddie jumped away fast from the rosy-cheeked kitchenmaid as the two responsible citizens entered the common room at the Bear.

"Oh, it's you, at last," he said idly, beginning to whistle.

"Up to the same old tricks, eh, Neddie boy?" asked Abe, shaking hands with the rather hot and quivering juvenile, with the quite hopeless tangle of black curls and the even less trustworthy eyes.

"It's all the plays, Abe, all the plays they have in London, weakened my will," Ned explained, slapping the reverend alderman and high bailiff on the paunch. Watching with some apprehension, Elder Brother saw a foolish smile twist up the grave lawyer's beard, and heard a chuckle.

"Oh, you boys around the Inns of Court now, and the playhouses, think you've seen better and done better than we did in my time. Thankee, Willy, no, I'll sit here, for my sciatica. Now, tell us, Neddie my lad, who pulled your fellows' playhouse down?"

"Have we ordered yet? My ears have not informed my brain what we have ordered yet," Ned said, looking nearly as smooth, benevolent and wise as his famous brother did, when he worked at it carefully.

"Ah, Millie dear, bring us some of that rare Spanish sack we got from . . . you know who, girl. And a good rare rib of beef, there's the girl."

Abe turned expectantly toward Ned.

Elder Brother also waited.

"Who pulled the great old Theatre down? Is that the question before the court?" Ned asked.

"It is, boy. That's it."

"Was it Topcliffe? Was it Gardiner? Who was it?" Shakespeare asked.

Young Ned leaned back comfortably against the pleasantly padded red leather of the bench, and beamed at them both. "Why, of course *we* did," he answered.

Their eyes stared and their mouths opened.

Shakespeare looked at Abe, and Abe looked at him.

"Never mind the drink, never mind the drink, you'll have your drink, tell us all about it," Ned's responsible brother ordered, trembling a little too much to be a picture of equanimity any longer.

"It was a cold, dark, windy night with a spit of snow in the air," began Ned, smacking his lips over some good salted herring. "And I said to Dick Burbage, when the news came that our lease had expired, I said, 'Dickie, old boy, let us hire ten great waggons, and twenty strong men, and take our trusty carpenter, old Peter Street, and go there in dark and dead of night, to Shoreditch, when the Watch is sleeping, and pull the damned thing down, piece by piece, and load it on our waggons, and transport it over London Bridge to the Bankside. And there —'"

"Yes? Yes?" shouted Sturley and Shakespeare.

"Ah, let me fill your cups, boys," said Ned, beginning to pour the smuggled Spanish sweet wine in a long purple shining spout, not spilling a drop either. "Where were we?"

"You were telling Dickie, the owner, what to do with the fragments of his playhouse," said Ned's patient brother, or seeming patient brother.

"Oh, yes. Neat little wine this. I've sat with more than one officer back from Cadiz while we split a bottle no better than this. Well, Dick said one thing, Tom Pope said another, but with old Burbage dead, and Cobham at his last gasp —"

"Oh, hell, I hate the way my brother breaks news," Shakespeare cried. "Is old Burbage dead then? And Cobham fading?"

"We'll hear me on mortuary matters as we ride to Oxford," Ned said soothingly, in his brother's best manner when he was arranging something for someone else to do before quite knowing it. "The long and the short of it is, boys, we loaded up our waggons that very night and transported it all to our land beyond Francis Langley's rents, in the best bloody place for a playhouse in Southwark, and with a little more money, and two or three new plays written to tempt the Queen and her fire-new and perfect Lord Chamberlain, I think we will put up such a lovely house as never yet has been seen in England. More beef, Abe, old boy. You eat well here, better than we have been doing without any help to speak of from this brother who left us."

William the Elder shook his head as though coming up out of deep water.

"Forgive me, Abe, for not knowing which end of my business is up, until I have it upended by this brother here, whom I thought I taught what I knew."

"The boy's just like thee, Willy, when the whole town and surrounding country used to wait, yea, and tremble, to see what madness would be next." Abe grinned with appreciation over those horrible precious days.

"Any more of this wine?" Ned asked in surprise.

"Millie! Another one of the good bottles!" Abe called.

"It is merciful that I am riding back to London with this absorber and consumer, before your supplies are gone," said the patient, indeed patient Shakespeare.

Ned's jaw dropped. "Oh, Willy, Willy, is it true?"

"Good, good, it will do you good, Willy, I think you have been restless a little here, lately. It will give you opportunity to see her Majesty and persuade her to soften the Privy Council and the justices toward the poor players. And we'll be waiting to welcome your company here, mind that, when it comes next summer. And then too, your tithes, Willy, and your daughters —"

"My daughters? What of my daughters?" Shakespeare's eyes were getting a little glazed.

"Why, they must marry, and add to their fine estate. Now we can do a bit of business on those fair parcels of yard-land out Snitterfield way. Can we not, Willy? Eh?"

Kneading his knobbly hands again.

"This indeed is a lovely sweet wine," Ned declared, taking the bottle neatly from the hands of the rosy girl, but still holding the hands until he had kissed her. "How well it loosens up words!"

"And that is not all, neither," Shakespeare murmured.

"I thought it would loosen up all those brave words that have been piling up in you, Willy, until, boom! They would come out in a brace of plays. Hey, Willy?"

"Hey Willy is right," said Ned's elder brother, holding onto the edge of the table. "Let me see. A new Lord Chamberlain. Let us have that on this bottle, shall we? Pray Bacchus it will not take a bottle apiece, until all thy well-bottled news is out."

"Oh, what a good idea!" said Ned, putting his feet up and leaning back like a traveller in one of the new coaches with padded seats, in preparation for a long, luxurious journey.

"Neddie, you shall play Brainworm. I promise. We have to beg some lord or justice to get poor Ben out of prison, and then rehearse his play of humours with the new actors."

"Abe, you're a magistrate, one of the longest-eared magistrates in the kingdom," said Ned, pouring him some of the smuggled wine. "I believe that you heard a holy promise from the brother who, I confess, I have trusted with my sacred body and my pure mind, no matter what wicked words he might in the past have written for this tender tongue to speak. You have heard him, Abe?"

"And golden words he speaks, and has ever spoken," said Abe Sturley, looking properly magisterial while big tears came into his eyes.

"Then let us for God's sake be going, for glory waits us on the boards of the new Globe, and will not be long kept waiting," Ned said, pouring the last cupfuls of the good wine. "Tell me, Willy, who'll play Lorenzo? Who'll play the old bald man in the play?"

Shakespeare arose and bowed to them both.

"That old bald man you see before you."

The sober, or reasonably sober tradesmen at the big centre table in the common room heard cheering from the small table in the corner.

"What's the news, boys?" called old Tom Barber to Abe Sturley.

"London matters, Court matters that can't be told yet," Abe said, looking dignified, like a high bailiff, which he was.

"There's to be a new playhouse in London, and I hear from this hairy young man here, who tells me everything I know, that its name is to be the Globe," said Shakespeare as the three eaters and drinkers went for their cloaks.

"Ah, a good name," Tom Barber said. "Is it any company you know, Willy, that will play in it?"

"The best of them are but shadows, but I think this one will, if it has protection, be the best."

"Oh, it will have good protection," Ned said softly into his ear. "Oh, Willy, nothing can stop us now. Old Hunsdon's son George will be new Lord Chamberlain, and we're to be his men as soon as I bring you back with me and prove it to him. He wants a new Falstaff play for his Garter feast."

A long, sad, reproachful look from Shakespeare. Innocent Neddie beamed back.

"So they sent you to fetch me, little by little, piece by piece, news by news, nose by nose."

"Willy, Willy, how can we wait a minute longer? Think of it, me as Brainworm! I'll crack Ben's jests like horse-beans."

"So I am afraid," said Shakespeare, as all three went out into Bridge Street among the cries of butchers, leather-sellers, and peddlers of goat-meat at their stalls and their barrows.

The round and ruddy sun, just sinking to rest over the peaceful Avon, beamed in their eyes like the oldest and best friend this earth ever had.

"A fine day for riding to Oxford tomorrow, lads," said High Bailiff Sturley, very imposing in his robe with three rows of very good beaver.

"I think we had better stop this side of Oxford," muttered the thoughtful Shakespeare.

"Why? The hostess at the Crown admires me, and treats me with the kindness my trusty heart doth yearn for," said his brother with nearly plausible sincerity.

Shakespeare did not answer anything in particular at that point, being occupied with a visitation of voices, strange voices and yet familiar, new and yet old too, like friends in new guises and altered accents. And with the voices, faint trumpets on the sweet wind blowing over the beloved river.

Oh, what a prince, if he had lived! And what a prince he will be, in memory of my boy!

Louder now to his stirring mind came the ringing cry of trumpets upon the battlements of Elsinore.

I'll do it. This time I'll do it. They cannot stop me from doing it.

Hamlet it shall be this time, whatever they say. Upon that royal trunk I'll graft my own fair and lovely bough, untimely blighted.

And in that wild and savage ground I'll plant the gentlest soul that was ever born.

In what weather? On how dark a night?

It shall be bitter cold. A quiet watch. Not a mouse stirring.

What hour now?
I think it lacks of twelve.
No, it is struck.
Indeed? Then it draws near the season
Wherein the Spirit held his wont to walk . . .

He returned to the shouting of butchers and leather-sellers in the muddy street.

"Abe, did you speak?"

Ned was nudging the high bailiff and muttering, "He has his spells at times. Best not pay any notice."

"Willy, there's much we can do here for your new and moral plays. Now that our corporation has set its face the right and level way, it may be other towns will follow us. I'll send letters to Warwick, Kenilworth, Coventry. . . . And there always will be Oxford —"

"Oh, no, not Oxford."

"Why, man? They love thee at Oxford."

"Let us think of those who love me here," said Shakespeare.

It was the same with those who loved him here. They calmly expected him to continue as a scribbler of stage plays for years and years to come; after he had reformed, after he had changed, after he had put all that behind him.

"Oh, that's good, Willy," Anne said, beaming at him proudly. "For the Queen herself! Think of that."

"But I'll be away again! Back in that scurvy old town of London, with its foul and infected air, away from my wife, and my daughters, and my house, and my roses —"

"Oh, Willy, but that's what you do," Anne said, patting his cheek and nodding with all the pride of an indulgent mother, who knows and is prepared for everything. "Think all the surprises we'll have to show you, when you come back!"

"Let us not show me too many, let us not show me too many," he said, but could not help smiling at the picture of the busy, abstracted wife, her mind half with her brewing and distilling, and with who knows what other great, astonishing things about, and around, and in and out of this wonderful house of hers!

The best house in Stratford! or with enough planning, and restoring, and renovation, and care, and especially with enough money, it surely would be, in the time to come.

"Oh, that will be fine, darling," said Mary, his mother, who might have made something pleasingly pathetic, if not tragic, about this eternal going and coming of his. Oh, no, not at all. "It will give us the chance to do something with our arms," she added, first looking cautiously over her shoulder to see that her husband was not creeping up to overhear what that woman was plotting to buy *now*.

The son looked at his mother, so grandly dressed, so splendidly the mistress of her substantial household, with all its servants, as befitted her station.

"Oh, it is fine enough for him, this silver falcon of his, but Willy, darling, never forget that our ancestors were Ardens, who were lords of this land before any Shakespeares were heard of — no matter how loud they talk at times —"

Hark! Was that the old man muttering in his shop? No, he was laughing, over some old tale he had probably told the same customer last week, or last month, or last year.

"They'll do it for thee, Willy, quarter our arms with the ancient arms of the Ardens. Or better still, impale them, one with the other. How handsome it will look! I can see it now, in gold, as it was for generations and for generations before us, the *ermine fess checky* of our poor martyred cousin, Edward Arden of Park Hall, and it will be again, my dear, when the heralds restore it to us, as they must surely do. Shall you have a coach? Anne should have a coach, when the girls are invited to great houses . . ."

Her fine eyes sparkled; her nostrils dilated; she tossed her head like a high-mettled mare.

Her eldest son, who had expected, or at least hoped for

some few tears, or at the very least some words of sorrow at this hard fate of his, always to be riding back and forth to sinful London, found himself thinking dark and gloomy thoughts about the vanity of human wishes, and the hollowness of human hopes, as if he had been a preacher, and not a writer of plays, for what, it now seemed, would be the rest of his mortal life.

But he held his tongue, and let his mother's happy prattle run on; and even nodded from time to time, as indulgently as Anne had nodded, when he was speaking.